JACQUELINE WOODSON

If You Come Softly

AND

Behind You

PUFFIN BOOKS
An Imprint of Penguin Group (USA) Inc.

JACQUELINE WOODSON

If You Come Softly

The title and the poem "If You Come Softly" by Audre Lorde are from *The Collected Poems of Audre Lorde* published by W. W. Norton and reprinted by permission of the Charlotte Sheedy Literary Agency.

PUFFIN BOOKS
Published by the Penguin Group
Penguin Young Readers Group, 345 Hudson Street, New York, New York 10014, U.S.A.
Penguin Group (Canada), 90 Eglinton Avenue East, Suite 700,
Toronto, Ontario, Canada M4P 2Y3 (a division of Pearson Penguin Canada Inc.)
Penguin Books Ltd, 80 Strand, London WC2R 0RL, England
Penguin Ireland, 25 St Stephen's Green, Dublin 2, Ireland (a division of Penguin Books Ltd)
Penguin Group (Australia), 250 Camberwell Road, Camberwell, Victoria 3124, Australia
(a division of Pearson Australia Group Pty Ltd)
Penguin Books India Pvt Ltd, 11 Community Centre,
Panchsheel Park, New Delhi - 110 017, India
Penguin Group (NZ), 67 Apollo Drive, Rosedale, North Shore 0632, New Zealand
(a division of Pearson New Zealand Ltd)
Penguin Books (South Africa) (Pty) Ltd, 24 Sturdee Avenue,
Rosebank, Johannesburg 2196, South Africa

Registered Offices: Penguin Books Ltd, 80 Strand, London WC2R 0RL, England

First published in the United States of America by G. P. Putnam's Sons,
a division of Penguin Young Readers Group, 1998
Published by Puffin Books, a division of Penguin Young Readers Group, 2010
This omnibus edition published by Puffin Books, a division of Penguin Young Readers Group, 2011

1 3 5 7 9 10 8 6 4 2

THE LIBRARY OF CONGRESS HAS CATALOGED THE G. P. PUTNAM'S SONS EDITION AS FOLLOWS:
Woodson, Jacqueline.
If you come softly / Jacqueline Woodson
p. cm.
Summary: After meeting at their private school in New York, fifteen-year-old Jeremiah,
who is black and whose parents are separated, and Ellie, who is white and whose mother
has twice abandoned her, fall in love and then try to cope with people's reactions.
ISBN: 978-0-399-23112-4 (hc)
[1. Interracial dating—Fiction. 2. Afro Americans—Fiction. 3. Family life—Fiction.
4. New York (N.Y.)—Fiction. 5. Schools—Fiction.]
I. Title
PZ7.W868If 1998 [Fic]—dc21 97-32212 CIP AC

Puffin Books ISBN 978-0-14-241522-1
This omnibus edition ISBN 978-0-14-241918-2

Printed in the United States of America

For the ones like Jeremiah

If You Come Softly

If you come as softly
as the wind within the trees
You may hear what I hear
See what sorrow sees.

My mother calls to me from the bottom of the stairs, and I pull myself slowly from a deep sleep. It is June. Outside the sky is bright blue and clear. In the distance I can see Central Park, the trees brilliant green against the sky. I was dreaming of Miah.

"Elisha," Marion calls again. She sounds worried and I know she is standing at the bottom of the stairs, her hand moving slowly up and down the banister, waiting for me to answer. But I can't answer yet. Not now.

Is there a boy? Marion asked me that fall, when Miah was new. And I lied and told her there wasn't one.

She is standing at the door now, her arms folded in front of her. "Time to get up, sweetie. Are you all right?"

I nod and continue to stare out the window, my hair falling down around my eyes, my pajamas hot and sticky against my skin.

No, Marion, there isn't a boy. Not now. Not anymore.

She comes to the bed and sits beside me. I feel the bed sink down with the weight of her, smell her perfume.

"I dreamed about Miah last night," I say softly, leaning my head against her shoulder. Outside, there are taxicabs blowing their horns. In the seconds of quiet between the noise, I can hear birds. And my own breathing.

Marion moves her hand over my head. Slowly. Softly. "Was it a good dream?"

I frown. "Yes . . . I think so. But I don't remember it all."

"Remember what you can, Elisha," Marion whispers, kissing me on the forehead. "Remember what you can."

I close my eyes again.

And remember what I can.

Part One

Chapter 1

JEREMIAH WAS BLACK. HE COULD FEEL IT. THE WAY THE sun pressed down hard and hot on his skin in the summer. Sometimes it felt like he sweated black beads of oil. He felt warm inside his skin, protected. And in Fort Greene, Brooklyn—where everyone seemed to be some shade of black—he felt good walking through the neighborhood.

But one step outside. Just one step and somehow the weight of his skin seemed to change. It got heavier.

Light-skinned brothers—well, yeah—sometimes he caught himself making fun of them. But everybody laughed. Everybody ragged on everybody.

Those same brothers—shoot!—they'd be getting on him just as hard. His homeboy—Carlton—messed-up name—Mama's white and Daddy's black, but he swears he's all black. Some days they'd be shooting hoops and Carlton'd just start going off on how black Jeremiah was. Nothing mean in it. It was all just the way they acted around each other. Sometimes they got to laughing so hard, tears'd be running down their faces. Laughing and pointing and trying to come up with something else funny to say. It was like that. When Jeremiah and his boys were hanging out, he just *was*. The way they all were. Some light-skinned, some dark-skinned, nappy-headed, curly-headed, even a couple *bald*-headed brothers—just hanging out and laughing. Those times, he felt free—like he was free inside his dark skin. Like he could celebrate it—throw his arms way out and grin.

Sometimes, he'd remember his grandma, a long time ago before the cancer took her—the way she'd make him sit in the shade. *Don't want you to get too black*, she'd say. He was little then and going back and forth between down south and Brooklyn. He didn't know anything back then. Back then, it was just his mama and daddy kissing him good-bye at the airport, Mama holding his hand so tight and for so long that he got embarrassed, then some stewardess taking his hand and sitting him right up front where she could keep a good eye on him like his mama had asked her to do. He remembered airplane wings, a pair of silver ones that a pilot gave him and his first whole meal on a little white plastic dish. There was always cake on the plane, real sweet cake, the kind his mama never let him eat at home. And then he'd fall asleep and be down south, and his grandma would be there waiting, already crying. She always cried when she saw him—cried and laughed all at once. Jeremiah smiled, remembering how he used to sink into her heavy arms and be surrounded by the smell of her rose-petal lotion.

That was a long time ago.

Jeremiah palmed his basketball in his left hand and held it straight out in front of him. He stared at it a moment then dribbled it three quick times against the curb. He wished his grandmother was alive so he could tell her—that it wasn't a bad thing. That you couldn't get *too* black. He remembered the time his father had taken him to see a film about the

Black Panthers—all those Afros and fists raised in the air. Jeremiah smiled. He wished his grandmother had heard them shouting *Black is beautiful.* But she hadn't. And she had believed what she said—that a person could get too black. The same way his father believed it every time he said, *Miah, you're a black man. You're a warrior.* But where was the fight? he used to wonder. Where was the war? Later on, when Jeremiah saw a cartoon about a monkey playing basketball, he felt ashamed, like that monkey was supposed to be him somehow. And he knew then, the war was all around him. It was people and commercials trying to make him feel like he didn't even matter, trying to make him feel like there was something wrong with being black.

And now, on the basketball court he always felt how black he was. It seemed as though he left his body and jogged over to the sidelines to watch himself. He saw the quads flexing under his dark thighs, saw his long brown arms reaching out for the ball, the way his calves moved as he flew down the court. He hated that he was gonna be playing ball for Percy Academy. No, it wasn't the game he hated, he loved that, had always loved that, couldn't remember a time when he didn't love the feel of the ball against his palms. But he hated that he would be playing it for Percy. White-bright Percy. At preseason practice, he'd look up sometimes and see all those white faces surrounding him. Yeah, there was Rayshon and Kennedy, they were black. Different though. Rayshon and Kennedy came from a different world. Yeah, they slapped each other five and gave each other looks when other teammates said something stupid. But at night, they went home to different worlds. Kennedy lived in the Albany Houses out in Brownsville. Rayshon lived in Harlem. Jeremiah frowned. He didn't want to be a snob.

I've been around the world, he thought. *I've been to India and Mauritius and Mexico. I'm different because of it. Different from them. Different from a lot of people—black and white.*

And he knew what was coming this winter—his first season on the team. He knew he'd look out at the stands and see more white faces—hundreds of them, cheering him and Percy Academy on. It seemed wrong—cliché somehow. Why couldn't he have loved tennis? Why hadn't someone stuck a racket or a golf club in his hand? Not like there was a golf course or tennis court anywhere near him— well, Fort Greene Park had courts, but you needed a permit and a partner. Basically, you needed to know something about the game before you could get it together to go there and play. And when he was real little, nobody was making a running leap for the tennis courts. But there was always some ball being played somewhere, a group of guys getting together in the park, someone setting an empty trash can on the curb for free throws, a fire escape ladder hanging down from somewhere with the rungs spaced just far enough apart for a basketball to fit through.

Jeremiah set the ball on the ground and stared at the back of his hand, at the place around his knuckles where the skin was darker than the rest of it. When he was little, his mama would always say, *Where's my beautiful brown-eyed, black baby child?* And he'd go running to her. *Right here,* he'd scream as she lifted him up high above her.

People were always telling him what beautiful eyes he had. Even strangers. Girls mostly. His eyes were light brown, almost green. He thought—had always thought—they looked strange against his dark skin. Sometimes he stared at himself in the mirror and wondered whether or not he was good-looking. Yeah, he knew girls checked him out all the time—but the pickin's were slim in Fort Greene, so they were probably just feeling desperate. *Black is beautiful. Don't get too black. Black monkey. Where's my beautiful black baby child. You're a black man. You're a warrior.*

Jeremiah sighed and stared out over the block. All the things people had always said to him—yeah, he'd heard them again and again. But sometimes, looking in that mirror, he had no idea who he was or why he was in this world.

And now, on top of everything, he had met a girl.

Chapter 2

IT RAINED THE AFTERNOON I MET JEREMIAH. A HARD, heavy rain that would last for four days. I walked home slowly in it, an umbrella I had bought on the street for three dollars barely keeping the rain off my back.

Our doorman, Henry, waved when he saw me then rushed forward, holding an oversized umbrella over mine. We had lived on Eighty-Eighth and Central Park West since I was a baby. And since I was a baby, Henry had been running out from his post by the door with an oversized umbrella to greet us when it rained. It didn't matter if we were carrying our own umbrellas.

I smiled at Henry. He was tall and quiet, with gray brown curly hair and skin so pale, you could see the veins running along his temples.

"First day in a new school, Ellie." Henry said.

I nodded. He never asked questions—just sort of stated things. "How can you tell?"

"The uniform. You're looking like me in it."

I glanced down at my Percy uniform, wondering if the administration knew the burgundy jackets and gray skirts we had to wear were the same colors that many doormen in the city had. "I guess I'll get used to it, huh?"

Henry winked at me. "You'll be surprised how quickly you do. Percy, right."

"I feel like I'm a walking billboard for that school," I said.

Henry laughed and returned to his post by the door. "I'll see you later, Ellie."

The elevator door slid open quietly. I stepped inside and waited for it to close, counting slowly under my breath. When it started moving again, I closed my eyes and thought about Jeremiah.

I had been staring at my program card, trying to figure out where room 301 or something was—

looking from the program card to the numbers on the doors and I had run right into him, my math and science textbooks crashing to the floor. Then he was apologizing and I was apologizing and we were both bending at the same time to retrieve them. And then—we just stopped and burst out laughing.

That's when he said his name—Jeremiah—and that stupid song about the bullfrog popped into my head so fast I just said it—"Like the bullfrog?"

"Yeah," he smiled. "Like the bullfrog."

I couldn't stop looking at him, at his smile and his hair. I had never seen locks up close. His were thick and black and spiraling down over his shoulders. I wanted to touch them, to touch his face. I wanted to hear him say his name again. For a moment we stared at each other, neither of us saying anything. There was something familiar about him, something I had seen before. I blinked, embarrassed suddenly, and turned away from him.

Then Jeremiah rose and I rose.

"Well . . . good-bye. I guess . . . I guess I'll see you around," he said softly, looking at me a moment longer before turning away and heading down the hall, his locks bouncing gently against his shoulders.

"Jeremiah," I whispered to myself as I walked away from him. I could feel his name, settling around me, as though I was walking in a mist of it, of him, of Jeremiah.

I stopped then and looked back over my shoulder. He was looking at me, a kind of puzzled look. *Jeremiah*, I thought, smiling. Jeremiah smiled back, then sort of waved, and turned into the classroom at the end of the hall.

Our apartment takes up the top two floors. Inside, it's more like a house than an apartment, with high windows, a fireplace in the living room, and stairs leading up to the bedrooms. I let myself in quietly then tiptoed up to my room. Outside, thunder clapped hard. The rain sounded soothing though, consistent. Like it would always come down. Like it would always be here.

I stepped out of my shoes by the closet then sat on the bed to peel off my wet socks. From my room, I could lie across my bed and watch the cars rush along Central Park West. In a hurry to get someplace. Everyone in New York is in a hurry. You see businessmen walking fast, their heads bowed, the cuffs of their pants flapping hard against their ankles. They don't look at anyone. Once I followed this man, walking so close beside him I could have been his daughter—but he never even looked over and noticed me. For two blocks I walked like that beside him. It made me sad for him—that he could walk through this world without looking left or right.

Lonely.

I sighed and lay back on my bed. Some people had friends surrounding them all the time. Sometimes when groups of girls passed by me, giggling and holding hands, my stomach tightened. I wanted that. But I didn't want that. Marion says it's because I was born so long after everybody else. The twins, Anne and Ruben, were already ten by the time I was born—and my older brother, Marc, and my sister, Susan, were in graduate school. She says I got used to being alone early on. And this house—with all its empty rooms and quiet. Some days I walked through it slowly, touching the walls of my sisters' and brothers' old rooms, wondering what it would feel like to grow up in a house full of people. And some afternoons, sitting at the coffee shop on the corner, eating fries and reading, I wanted to hug myself. Those days, being alone felt whole and right and good.

Jeremiah. Who did he go home to? Would he remember me? Had he seen it too, whatever *it* was that I saw when we looked at each other? What was it?

Once I had kissed a boy—a boy named Sam in seventh grade. He wore braces that made him lisp. Around me he was always nervous and fumbling, offering to carry my books and buy me sodas. I liked him, liked how he stuttered and looked away from me. One day I just kissed him, leaned forward while he was sitting beside me stuttering out a tale about his father's sailboat. I had never kissed anyone on the lips and Sam's lips felt dry and hard. But at the same time warm and sweet. We sat there, in the park, our lips pressed together until Sam pulled away. After that, he avoided me.

Lying across my bed, I wondered where he was now. Good old Sam, who grew scared of me suddenly, scared of kissing. I wondered when I'd kiss someone again. Wondered if it would be Jeremiah.

"Elisha!" my mother called from the bottom of the stairs. "Are you planning on spending the whole afternoon in that room?"

"Maybe," I yelled back.

I sat up and pressed my hand across the pleats of my gray Percy skirt before pulling it off. I had never worn a uniform. It had hung in my closet beneath thin dry-cleaning plastic all summer. Once I had tried it on for Marion and my father and they had smiled, made me turn this way and that. Still, it felt strange to walk into a school full of people dressed exactly like me.

"Elisha," Marion called again. "Come down and tell me about your first day."

I met a boy, I wanted to scream. *His name is Jeremiah.*

"I'm changing clothes, Marion. I'll be down for dinner."

"Well, it's almost dinnertime now."

In the dining room, Marion had set the table for two. A thin white candle melted slowly inside a silver holder. I stared at the flame a long time. Jeremiah's face flickered once inside of it, then disappeared.

There were rolls and a bowl of steaming green beans on the table. When I was small, I had gone for weeks eating only green beans. My parents laughed about it now, about how they had worried I'd wake up completely green one day.

"Daddy working?" I asked, coming up behind Marion in the kitchen.

In the past year, I had grown as tall as my mother. It was strange that in such a short time, she had gone from being someone I had to look up at to someone I met at eye level.

"Of course he's working," she said. "First I was married to a nice young medical student and I saw him all the time. Then I was married to a resident and I saw him once in a while. Now I'm married to a doctor who I never see. He called right before you got home from school—said he hoped your first day went well."

"It was fine. It's just like Jefferson only the kids can afford dermatologists." Thomas Jefferson was the public school I had transferred from.

Marion laughed. She pulled a chicken covered with rosemary and lemon slices from the oven.

"Smells good, Marion."

"Stop calling me Marion."

"Stop calling me Elisha."

"That's your name."

"And Marion's yours." I smiled, pulling a sprig of rosemary from the chicken. It had been going on like this for years. She refused to call me Ellie, so I refused to call her Mom.

"Goodness, I'm glad you're the last teenager I'll ever have to raise . . . *Elisha*. Even when you're fifty, you'll still be Elisha." She shook her head and looked at me. "What if we *had* named you Ellie. Kids would have called you 'Smelly' Ellie or 'Tattle-Telly' Ellie. You would have come home crying every afternoon."

I rolled my eyes. "You should have been a poet."

My mother smiled. "Go put the chicken on the table, silly."

I started pulling the sleeves of my sweatshirt down over my hands.

"Use pot holders, Elisha!"

"Yes, Marion. We don't want another little accident."

She laughed again and swatted me with the dish towel. It was a family joke. When the twins were still living at home, they would refer to me as our parents' little accident. Even though my mother and father swore they had planned to have another child, none of us believed them.

"It was the dancing," Marion said, following behind me with a bowl of mashed potatoes. She set them carefully on the table. "If your father hadn't taken me out dancing that night—we went to Roseland—maybe, then maybe, you wouldn't be here. But it was the dancing and, possibly, the wine." She winked at me and sat down.

I sat across from her. "I'm sure it had a lot to do with the wine."

"And a lot to do with why I haven't touched a drop since!"

We laughed and the laughter seemed to echo through the empty house and wind its way back to us. We were almost friends now.

A long time ago, Marion left us. Just packed up and was gone. I was little and the twins were still living at home then. The three of us cried every night for a week while my father took time off from medical school to try to find her. Then we stopped crying, and three weeks later she returned.

When she left the next time, I was eight and the twins had left for college. I was old enough to understand what it meant that she wasn't coming home for a while, that she might never come home. When she did, I couldn't speak to her for a long time. Scared to say the wrong thing. Scared she'd leave again.

When you're young and your mother leaves, something inside of you fills up with the absence of her. I don't know how to explain. For a long time, there was this place inside of me where love for Marion should have been but wasn't.

"Marc called," Marion said, tearing a chicken leg away with her hands. I watched her, saying nothing. There were parts of her that were still, even after all these years, unfamiliar to me. The way her hands moved when she ate. The way she brushed her hair down over her eyes before sweeping it back behind her ears. "He said the girls are safely tucked away at boarding school."

My oldest brother's daughters were twelve. All summer, he and his wife had been calling. His wife wanted the girls to go to boarding school and Marc didn't. The twins didn't know what they wanted.

"Good riddance." I didn't like my nieces. They were spoiled and prim. Even at twelve, they insisted on dressing identically. There was something weird about that to me. It's one thing to have someone in the world who looks *exactly* like you—I mean, that part you can't help. But to want to *dress* exactly like that person was a different story.

Marion shook her head. "It's not like you'll see them any less, Elisha."

"I know. One can only hope."

Marion laughed.

Although they lived in Seattle, they came east once a year at Hanukkah. Unfortunately, that would probably still be the case whether they were at boarding school or not.

"One day I'll join Marc and Susan and Anne and Ruben on the great parental divide." I smiled, picked up a green bean with my fingers and chewed it slowly.

My sisters and brothers had all moved on a long time ago. I missed my sister Anne the most. Sometimes we spent hours on the phone talking about nothing really. She would probably have all kinds of things to say about Jeremiah. Anne was like that. She had an opinion about everything and everyone whether she'd met them or not. She had opinions about the *idea* of things.

"So do you love it or hate it?"

I blinked. I didn't love him, I didn't even *know* him.

"Excuse me?"

My mother raised her eyebrows. "Well *someone* was far away."

"I was thinking."

"About what?"

I looked down at my plate. "Nothing."

My mother sighed. "Don't say 'nothing,' Elisha. You don't have to tell me. Just don't lie about it. Say 'none of your business.' "

"None of your business." I put another green bean in my mouth.

"Does it involve a boy?"

"None of your business."

"You're too young for boys, Elisha. Do you want a glass of water?"

"Water instead of a boyfriend?" I smiled. "No thank you."

Marion got up and went to the kitchen. A few minutes later, she came back with two glasses brimming with water and ice and set one beside my plate.

"There. Cool your thirst."

I pulled a piece of chicken from its bone with my fingers, ignoring the glass of water. "If I were interested in boys," I said slowly. "Which I am not. What would be the *appropriate* age?"

Marion was thoughtful for a moment. "I guess seventeen or eighteen."

"You were *married* at eighteen, Marion. And pregnant. And I'm not even going to venture a guess as to which one happened first."

"Things were different then," she said slowly, concentrating on cutting a piece of chicken and putting it in her mouth.

"Well, they're different now."

She chewed for a moment and swallowed. When she spoke again, her voice was low and even. "Elisha Eisen—you're in the tenth grade. Math, science, English, and a few girlfriends to have some tea or a slice of pizza with once in a while. That's tenth grade. Ask anyone."

"You're living in the fifties, Marion."

"You've got years and years for boys." Her eyes were sad when she said this.

"You don't know that," I said, getting angry. "You don't know what's going to happen tomorrow or the next day. You don't know if I have years and years."

"Trust me . . . Ellie . . ."

I shook my head. "Trust me . . . Mom . . . you don't know."

My mother was quiet for a moment. When she spoke again, her voice was shaky, unsure. "I know I don't know, Elisha. But I do know if you rush into your life, you miss things sometimes."

I shrugged, looking away from her, embarrassed suddenly. She had married young, and some mornings I came down to the kitchen to find her staring out of the window, a dazed look in her eyes.

"You felt like we just kept coming, didn't you?" I said. "And you just kept getting further and further away from your life."

She put her fork down. "You kids *are* my life," she said.

"But we weren't always."

"I didn't know I'd wake up one day and not be able to go run a quarter mile in under a minute." She sighed, pushing a few stray hairs back behind her ears. "That my legs would hurt from just the mere act of throwing them over the side of the bed."

"You left us," I said.

I had not known I was going to say this. I hadn't wanted to. I had wanted to ask what it felt like to be old, to be wishing for things you couldn't ever have again.

Outside, the rain was falling steadily, drumming against the windowpane. I turned to watch it for a moment. It was almost night, and the sky was caught in the silvery in-between place that made a person's throat hollow out.

"I left you," Marion said softly, her voice catching. "I left my family. And you—my baby girl. Isn't that a terrible thing?" After a moment, she added, "Yes. Yes, it is. A terrible thing."

I turned away from the window. I wasn't hungry anymore. Everything felt hot and tight. I wanted to be upstairs alone in my room, with the door closed. I didn't want this—to talk about this—this *thing* nobody ever said a word about. But now that we were talking, I couldn't stop.

"You left us broken all open," I said. "All reeling, Marion. I didn't know it back then . . ." I felt a lump forming in the back of my throat. It could have been yesterday that we discovered her gone. It could have been an hour ago. "I was only a little kid. I didn't know I was reeling. Anne stood at the refrigerator for an hour wondering what you would cook if you were here. You didn't know that, did you?"

Marion shook her head. She looked small and beaten suddenly. No one ever talked about what it was like. And she never asked. Just walked back in one afternoon and held her arms out, ready for us to jump into them.

And I did the first time. But Anne and Ruben hung back, leaning back against the counter with their hands in their pockets, watching her.

"An *hour*, Marion—while me and Ruben sat at the table, hungry. Hungry and struck dumb. And Daddy upstairs calling all the places he thought you might be . . ." I swallowed. "Nobody knew where to begin."

I folded my hands on the table. When Marion reached out with her own to touch them, I snatched them back. I didn't want her to touch me. Not now.

"We were like, I don't know—like *holes* or some-thing—just all . . . all empty and lost. And that first night, we were so . . . so hungry."

Marion sighed and looked away from me. "You're

fifteen, Elisha," she said slowly. "You have no idea what it's like. No idea."

"We thought you were dead."

"I *was* dead. In here." She pointed to her chest. "I woke up that morning knowing I wouldn't be able to stand another day of making breakfast and lunch and dinner, of fixing arguments between you all, of listening to Edward fret over medical school—of all the noise and mess and . . ." Her voice drifted off. When she started speaking again, she was whispering. "I had to go."

I stared down at my hands. "Then why'd you come back?"

"Because I couldn't live without those same things I couldn't live *with*."

I swallowed. I would never trust her. Not one hundred percent. Not the way some people can trust their mothers.

"You know what it made me realize, Marion? That you wouldn't always be here. That I can't take anything or anyone for granted 'cause there's no guarantee."

Marion reached out for my hand again. This time I let her take it.

"I wish you were thirty and realizing that. Or forty. Or even twenty-five. I wish you didn't have to realize it at fifteen. As for me, I haven't left in seven years and don't think I will again."

We didn't say anything for a long time. I turned back toward the rain. One day someone *would* be here for me—and I wouldn't take that person for granted.

"Tell me about him," Marion said, a small smile at the corners of her lips. "Tell me about this boy."

I shook my head, feeling relieved, glad the conversation about leaving was over for now. "No."

"Does he go to temple?"

I laughed. I knew she was teasing. *We* rarely went to temple. "If there was a boy—which there isn't—I don't think he'd go to temple." I tried to imagine Jeremiah with a yarmulke, his locks springing out around it.

Marion smiled. "I guess that's what happens when we send you to a gentile school. How do you like it?"

I shrugged. "It's okay. It's not Spence or Dalton or Nightingale-Bamford. It's Percy. The kids look like their daddies are rich and their mothers are good-looking."

"Is this boy's daddy rich?"

I pressed my fork into the mashed potatoes. They were lumpy and thin, the way they always were. It was the one thing my mother couldn't do well. "There . . . is . . . no . . . boy . . . Marion."

"Well, you'll meet some nice friends there. And maybe in your junior year, there'll be a boy."

I had chosen Percy myself—from a dozen schools—because I liked the name. It made me think of that song "When a Man Loves a Woman" by Percy Sledge. I knew it was a stupid reason to choose a school, but they all seemed exactly alike.

"I had nice friends at Jefferson."

Marion and my father had decided to send me to private school in May, when the *New York Times* reported that Thomas Jefferson had the lowest reading levels and college acceptance rate in all of New York City.

"But none of those friends will get into college," Marion said.

"The only reason Percy has a ninety-eight percent college acceptance rate is because the kids are rich. Their parents *buy* them good grades."

Marion frowned. "That doesn't happen."

I shrugged. "Maybe."

"No one can *buy* you a high SAT score, Elisha. No one can *buy* you a high reading level."

I raised an eyebrow at her and smiled. "Things have changed, Marion."

All of my brothers and sisters had gone to Jefferson High. And from there, they had all gotten into decent universities. When I argued this, my mother said, *That was a long time ago, before we had money to send you to private school. Things have changed.*

"Not that much," she said now, rising to clear the table. "I made some apple tarts for dessert. Your favorite. Maybe in your junior year you can have the boy over for tarts and tea."

I handed her my plate. "Marion," I said. "If—"

"I know, I know, Elisha. If there was a boy, which there isn't, he wouldn't be apple tart and tea kind."

Chapter 3

HE LOVED THE LIGHT IN HIS MAMA'S KITCHEN. THE yellow stained-glass panes across the top of the windows buttered the room a soft gold—even now, in the early evening with the rain coming down hard outside.

"Your daddy left a message," his mama said. "Said he had to go out to L.A. Be back Sunday night. Left a number."

"Guess I'm spending the week here then." Jeremiah glanced out the kitchen window. There was no light on in his father's apartment. He was glad he didn't have to make a decision. Every night it was the same thing. *You gonna stay here? You gonna stay here?* His mama and daddy's voices beating against the side of his head, begging him as if they were really saying, *Choose me. No, choose me.* For the hundredth time, no, maybe the thousandth time, he wished he had a brother or sister—somebody to go up against them with. Someone to help relieve some of the stuff they put him through. How long would it have to be like this anyway? Two addresses. Two phone numbers. Two *bedrooms*.

Jeremiah sighed and sat down at the kitchen table and watched his mama fuss with pots and pans. She was making spaghetti sauce—the way they liked it with lots of peppers and onions and no meat. A long time ago, she'd given up red meat. Little by little Jeremiah gave it up too. Every once in a while, he found himself craving a burger with ketchup and mayo the way he used to like it. But it had been a long time since he'd eaten one. It would probably make him sick to his stomach now. He let his basketball roll back and forth between his feet for a few minutes then kicked it gently into the corner.

"You hungry?"

Jeremiah nodded. The kitchen smelled like garlic and tomatoes. "I guess so."

His mother looked at him a moment. She was

pretty—his mama was. He'd always thought so. She wore her hair short, tied her head up with pretty scarves. Tonight she was wearing an orange and yellow one, wrapped high like a turban. Her skin was dark like his and smooth. People said they had the same mouth—wide and soft. And the same eyes. His eyes were light brown like hers and people were always asking them if they were wearing contact lenses. Now his mother smiled, shaking her head. She pressed her fingers to her lips.

"What?" Jeremiah said, feeling his own face break into a smile. This evening, his mama was wearing jeans and a T-shirt with Vassar printed across the front. She had gone there, had studied literature and film. The summer after she graduated, she took a film course at NYU that his father was teaching. She had heard of him—had even seen a couple of his movies. They dated a long time before they married. *I wanted to be sure he was the right man,* his mother used to say.

She didn't have much to say about his daddy anymore.

"You gonna tell me how your first day was or am I going to have to guess."

"You gonna have to guess," Jeremiah said.

His mother turned back to the stove and stirred the sauce once more. Jeremiah watched her lift spaghetti from the colander onto the blue plates they always ate off. The plates had been a wedding gift from his grandmother—his father's mother. Sometimes the memory of her crept up quickly— unexpected—like somebody sneaking up behind you in the dark. He missed his grandmother more than anything. In February it would be five years since she passed. Jeremiah twirled the saltshaker absently, wondering how long it took before you stopped missing someone.

"I was thinking about Grandma just now," he said.

"Yeah? What were you thinking?"

"Just about her. She came into my mind." He bit his bottom lip. "Remember that time she was interviewed about Daddy?"

His mama smiled. It was a sad smile, full of good and bad memories. Jeremiah was sorry he had even started talking about his grandma. Sometimes he forgot that Grandma was his father's mother.

Mama put the plates of spaghetti down on the table. "Which time?" she asked.

"I don't remember the show. I think it was around the time of the first Oscar nomination. Remember, she wore that bright red dress and that silly necklace I'd made her—the one made out of bottle tops?"

His mama smiled.

"She said that even though he was a big-time moviemaker, she had changed his diapers and she could tell everyone listening that Daddy's poop smelled just as bad as anybody else's. Later on, she'd told me she wanted to use the other word, but it would have gotten bleeped out and she wanted to make sure the American audience got the message."

"I thought Norman was going to lose it for sure."

"Me and Grandma laughed about that for a long time," he said softly.

Jeremiah ran his fingers slowly across the table. Outside he could hear little girls singing, "*Miss Lucy had a baby, she named him Tiny Tim . . .*" He swallowed. When he had looked into that girl's eyes today, he saw something familiar in them. A little bit of himself there. Where was she now?

"Want some wine, high-school boy?" She poured a glass of red wine for herself and waited.

Jeremiah sighed, knowing his mama was trying to change the subject. *I miss you, Grandma. You would be able to tell me, wouldn't you? You'd be able to make everything all right.*

"Pinot Noir," she said. "Supposed to be a good vintage—1993 from the Napa Valley."

Before they separated, his mother and father had gone to the wine country. When they came home, his mama filled him in on everything she'd learned about wine, and together they sat sipping various wines and comparing them. He wasn't really allowed to drink yet, but his mother still offered and told him everything she knew about certain wines. She said she wanted him to be knowledgeable when the time came to choose one.

"Nah. 1993 wasn't great for Pinot Noirs. If you had a Cabernet or even a Petite Syrah then maybe."

His mama smiled.

They were quiet for a moment. Jeremiah watched her dance a hot loaf of bread from the oven to the table and wondered again how his father could have just fallen for someone else. Yeah, over and over, his father had tried to explain it to him, and each time Jeremiah thought he finally understood. But then

he'd come home some evening and find his mother
sitting in front of the television in the empty living
room and his heart would tighten inside his chest.
She looked lonely and lost sitting in the half-light.

"Mama? You ever planning on writing another
book?"

It seemed a long time ago when he would come
home to find her writing in her study. She had written three novels and had always said she wanted to
write ten in her lifetime. And for a while, Jeremiah
thought she'd do it. But after his father left, she had
stopped writing and Jeremiah rarely found her in
her study anymore.

She sat down across from him and frowned.
"What makes you ask that?"

Jeremiah shrugged. "Just wondering."

"Well, eat instead of wondering." After a moment, she said, "It takes time, you know."

"But you have lots of time and I . . . I just never
see you in the study anymore."

"I haven't felt much in the mood for writing anything lately." She glanced at him then back down at
her plate, drumming her fingers on the table the
way she did when she was annoyed. "When you

have so much *real* drama in your life, it's hard to think about fiction. I'm taking some me time now. Figure with what I have saved and this house being paid for and Norman paying for your school, we'll be okay." She reached across the table and covered his hand with her own. "Okay, honey?"

Jeremiah nodded but didn't say anything.

Some mornings he woke up remembering little things—like the way his father's arm looked when it was draped across his mama's shoulder or his father and mother hugging by the kitchen sink, the water still running from the dishes one of them had been washing.

He wondered where that stuff went to, where love went to, how a person could just love somebody one day and boom—the next day love somebody else.

"Tell me about Percy, Miah."

"It's okay. You know. It's a school. Uniform's really the only thing makes it much different from Tech. It's whiter. Much whiter. But I figured that."

"They think you're on scholarship?"

Jeremiah shrugged and stared down at his plate. "Nobody said anything stupid."

"Some people going to think that, you know. Don't let them get to you."

"I won't—I mean, I know. But I kind of rather have them think that than know the truth, right?"

His mother nodded. "Yeah, honey—but it's okay if they know the truth. I'm not saying you have to strut it. But you don't have to be ashamed of it either."

The truth was he was Norman Roselind's son. And anyone who had ever stepped foot inside a movie theater or picked up a paper knew who Norman Roselind was. Yeah, he was proud of his father and the movies he'd made. But sometimes he just wanted to be Miah. And the truth was, his mother had gotten a lot of attention for her three books— you said her name, Nelia Roselind, and people knew it. Norman and Nelia—they had even been on the cover of a couple of magazines. One magazine had called them "most romantic." Jeremiah twirled the spaghetti around on his fork. He wondered what the magazines would say now—or what they had already said. A long time ago, he had stopped reading them, too afraid to find some nasty gossip about his family somewhere between their pages.

"I walk into Percy and it's like I can reinvent myself or something, you know? Without Daddy's movies and your books. Just me."

"Well, don't go reinventing yourself too much. It's okay to be our son. Remember Brooklyn Tech—people knew who you were there and you got along fine."

"Yeah, I remember." At Tech, some people treated him strange and some people treated him okay. His homeboys, the guys he'd grown up with, they were cool, had always been cool. But new kids, well, sometimes they just acted *weird*, like he was some untouchable *god* or something. He hated that.

If things had turned out different, he would have stayed at Tech. If this. If that. Would his life always be filled with "ifs?" If his parents were still together. If Lois Ann had never been born. If that girl had told him her name.

Percy Academy was one of the most expensive schools in New York City. Nobody knew if that meant it was one of the best. Jeremiah didn't think so. It had been his father's idea. Jeremiah would have been fine staying at Brooklyn Tech, which was right in the hood and where he'd gone to ninth grade. Or even Stuyvesant. He knew some brothers there. But his father had insisted on a private school, talking about Jeremiah being his only son and all and wanting the best for him. Jeremiah had finished his first year at Tech, had made the varsity team and gotten straight A's. Then summer came and his father moved across the street and started talking about better schools. Jeremiah knew it was his guilt talking. But he wanted to make his daddy happy too.

One Friday afternoon, his father showed up at the door talking about taking Jeremiah on a tour of Percy, a school he'd read about in the *Times*. Jeremiah looked down at his plate of spaghetti now, remembering how quickly he climbed into his daddy's car. That afternoon, when he looked up at his window, his mama was standing there, looking down at them. It was the beginning of choosing between them. He'd gone to Percy for his daddy—but everything else, not eating meat, coming to her house first after school, not cursing or acting the fool (too much)—that was for Mama.

The guy who showed them around had gone on and on about the small classes and how Jeremiah would "blossom" in such an environment. Like he was some sort of flower or something. *A rose is a rose is a rose is a Jeremiah Roselind.* That's what his mother used to say to him when he was little. That was a long time ago. Now he was fifteen. Fifteen. Sixteen was probably something, but fifteen—fifteen was a place between here and nowhere.

"Earth calling Miah." His mama was snapping her fingers in front of his face. Jeremiah smiled and took a big forkful of spaghetti.

"Coach there used to play for the Knicks. Way back in the day. Said even before he saw me play he'd heard about my game from Coach Thomas."

His mother raised her eyebrows and smiled. "Thomas called him?"

Jeremiah nodded. Thomas had coached him at Tech, but he went further back than that. He and Jeremiah's mama had dated in high school.

"Coach said they've been waiting for a point guard to get to Percy for years." He smiled. "You think Thomas laid it on kind of thick?"

"Thomas knows a good point guard when he sees one. And besides that, I don't think he'd be lying for me—not after all these years."

"And after you broke his heart."

His mother waved her hand at him. "We were just a couple of years older than you are now. Shoot! We've both had our hearts broken dozens of times since then. You'll see."

What was her name? That girl in the hallway with the thick black hair. And those pretty eyes. The way she'd looked at him. Then she looked back— over her shoulder. He was looking too, waiting to see if she'd tell him her name. He liked the way she looked at him. It was different. She didn't seem scared or anything.

"This is good." Jeremiah pointed his fork at the pasta.

His mama eyed him. "Listen to your good mood talking. You never say anything's good."

"I'm turning over a new leaf."

"That leaf must be some kind of pretty. What's her name?"

Jeremiah shook his head. Sometimes he felt like glass in front of his mama—like something she could look right through and see straight to the other side of.

"*Nobody*, Ma. I'm for real. I just like the spaghetti tonight."

"Well then—thank you. I'm glad you like it."

45

They laughed and ate silently for a few moments. It felt good tonight, sitting across from her. Easy. Later maybe, if the rain stopped, he'd go shoot some hoops with Carlton—find out what was happening at Tech. But right now, sitting in the kitchen like this was enough.

"They'll probably have you hitting those books pretty hard at Percy."

"I guess."

"You should give your daddy a call later on."

Jeremiah nodded, feeling the easiness leave him. "I will."

He hated this. Had hated it from day one. What kind of family lived across the street from each other? And this apartment—all nine rooms of it. His homeboys had always called it a little mansion. It seemed too big with just the two of them in it now, the guests' rooms and his daddy's empty study collecting dust. When he was still living here, his daddy had company all the time—people coming in from out of town for film shoots, friends from college who had moved to the West Coast, actors and directors. Somebody was always showing up and staying a night or two. There were pictures all over the house of Jeremiah with this actor or that director. His daddy was well known in the movie industry—his last movie had earned him two Oscar nominations. Jeremiah remembered how beautiful his mama looked in her gown and how handsome and happy his daddy was that night. His daddy had even taken him shopping for a tuxedo, and even though it felt stiff and strange, he felt grown-up walking along the red carpet in front of his parents.

"You talk to him lately?" Jeremiah asked now.

His mama looked annoyed. "I don't have boo to say to that man. And he doesn't have boo to say to me."

"Boo!" Jeremiah said. He was teasing but maybe not too. They were his parents and he was stuck with them in all of their ridiculousness. Almost a year now since his daddy moved across the street. And it wouldn't be so bad if he hadn't moved in with Lois Ann King, who Jeremiah had known almost all his life. For twelve years they'd been living on this block. And for twelve years Lois Ann had been living across the street. And now his daddy was living with her. He would never go over there if it wasn't for the stupid courts saying he had to spend equal time in both places.

"Soon as this slow-moving divorce is final—I'm sure he'll be moving out west anyway. He can take his Lois Ann and move to kingdom come for all I care."

"He's not gonna move out west," Jeremiah said softly.

His mother looked at him. "Don't be so sure, honey."

"He wouldn't leave me here and I wouldn't go with him." He pushed his plate of spaghetti away. He wasn't hungry anymore. Just tired. Tired of everything. Sometimes he wanted to scream—just stand in the middle of the street and holler. Three years and he'd be so far away from here, it was gonna leave everybody's head spinning.

But that was a whole three years away. Tomorrow, if he saw that girl, he was going to ask her name.

Chapter 4

THE PHONE RANG EARLY SATURDAY MORNING, A WEEK after school had started. I was lying in bed, my history book propped against my legs.

"Is anyone going to get it?" I called from my room. When no one answered, I swallowed, scared suddenly. Then I remembered Marion had said she was going shopping and my father was playing golf. I took the stairs two at a time and picked up the phone in the kitchen.

"Hello?"

"Hey baby-sis, it's Anne."

I leaned against the wall and exhaled. "Anne," I said softly.

"Is she not home?"

"Yeah." I lowered myself down against the wall until I was sitting. Anne knew. She always knew when I was afraid. Like she could look right through me—across all the miles—and see that place right there in the center of me where all the scared was. Maybe she felt it sometimes too—that Marion would take off again. Disappear.

"I don't think she's going to leave again, Ellie. I mean—it's been a long time."

I nodded then said, "Yeah," hoping Anne was right.

"Guess who came for dinner last night?"

"The Rubik cube," I said, smiling. We had called Ruben by this name for as long as I could remember.

"How'd you know?" Anne asked. I could hear the surprise and exasperation in her voice.

"He called Marion late last night."

"Did he tell her about the ceremony?"

"What ceremony?"

"Good, he didn't."

"*What* ceremony?" I asked again. In the background, I could hear dishes rattling and imagined

Anne in her kitchen in San Francisco making tea. For a while she only drank coffee, black and sugarless, the way Marion drank it. Then one day, she gave it up and moved on to herbal teas.

Now Anne took a sip of something. "Did I tell you I cut my hair? It kind of looks like Daddy's."

"Marion's gonna have a fit. Who's having a ceremony?"

"I think I'll dye it brown like yours. Maybe I'll perm it."

I smiled and shook my head. She was teasing me the way she always did. And I was taking the bait, the way *I* always did.

"I started Percy this week," I said casually.

"Don't you want to hear about the ceremony?"

I laughed. "No. Lost interest. Anyway, I need to talk to you about something."

"Me and Stacey are having a commitment ceremony."

Stacey was Anne's girlfriend. They had been together almost four years. When Anne first came out, Marion hit the roof. But by then, Anne was already living in San Francisco, so there wasn't a whole lot Marion could do. Anne had told me stories about parents who threw their kids out of the house or snatched them out of college.

"What are you guys committing to?"

"Not *what,* silly. Whom. We're committing to each other."

I rolled my eyes. "You've been together four years. Isn't that kind of *obvious?*"

I heard Anne exhale.

"It's obvious to me and Stacey, but we want the rest of the world to know too. You know—like a wedding but not with all that 'honor thy husband/protect thy wife' stuff."

"Are you guys wearing gowns or tuxedos—"

"No, Ellie," Anne said, sounding a bit too patient. "We're wearing regular clothes. Nice regular clothes. Anyway, I want you to come out to San Francisco for it. We haven't set a date yet. Maybe late January or early March. We're going to have a bunch of friends over and say some vows to each other. Ruben wasn't very keen on the idea. I figured he blabbed to Mom already."

"Nah. Marion would have said something. Just like she's going to say no about me coming out there in the middle of school."

"I'll talk to her. Would you come?"

"Of course, Anne. I *miss* you."

"I miss you too. Your turn, prep schooler. I can't believe an Eisen child is in prep school. What is this world coming to?" She laughed. I missed her laugh, the way the edges of her gray eyes crinkled with it.

I pulled a strand of hair into my mouth and chewed on it for a moment. Maybe one day me and Jeremiah would have a commitment ceremony. What vows would I make—that if we ever met for the first time in the hallway again, I'd remember to tell him my name?

"I don't really have anything. I mean not like yours."

"You met someone, didn't you?" I could tell she was smiling.

"Yeah. Kind of." I leaned my head back against the wall and closed my eyes.

"Boy or girl?"

"A boy." I smiled, relieved. "This guy named Jeremiah."

"Jeremiah," Anne said. "I like that. Like the bullfrog."

I laughed.

"What's his last name?"

"I don't know."

"Oh, you guys sound *real* serious."

I cradled the phone between my head and shoulder and started chewing on a cuticle. Outside, a baby was crying. I missed Anne sitting across the table from me, missed her pulling my ponytail every time she passed me. And other stuff too—the long-ago things, like how she'd read to me at night, tuck me in, and kiss that ticklish place right where my forehead stops and my hair begins.

"You think you'll ever move back to New York, Anne?"

"Don't try to change the subject."

"I'm not. I just wish you were here. I wish you could meet him."

Anne was quiet for a moment. "Tell me what's so special about him."

"I don't know. I mean, he probably doesn't even know I exist. I forgot to tell him my name when I met him. Isn't that silly? I'm—like obsessing about this guy and he doesn't even know my name."

"That's not silly. Something about him caught

you—off guard. It was like that with Stacey. I knew the first time she said a word to me that I'd want to spend my life with her. It's not silly. It's just—I don't know—another strange part of living. What does he look like?"

"Well, I only saw him once, really—we bumped into each other—literally. And he helped me pick up my books. And then he looked at me and smiled. And it was like something inside of me went crazy."

Anne laughed. "I bet I'd like him. Anybody who makes something inside of my stable baby sister go crazy must be amazing."

"He's taller than me," I said. "He has locks and these bright brown eyes—"

"Locks?"

"His hair. You know."

"Ugh. That's kind of a bummer."

"Why?"

"I don't like white guys with locks. I mean—it's so obviously an appropriation—"

"He's *black*, Anne."

She didn't say anything. I could feel the air between us getting weird. Maybe a minute passed. Maybe two.

"Really?"

"No," I said, growing annoyed. "I'm lying."

"Sorry, Ellie. I just thought Percy Academy was so chichi and *white*."

"Well, it isn't." I wanted her to say something different. Something smart—the way she always did.

We were silent.

"You're mad, aren't you?"

"No."

"Then what are you?"

I sighed. "Nothing. I gotta go. I have to study—"

"Ellie. Don't be like this. I'm just surprised, that's all."

"You were all excited before. Before I told you he was black."

"Well, I'm still excited. I can be surprised and excited at the same time. Geez. I just never thought about it—you know."

"Well, maybe you should ask yourself why. It's not like you don't see black people every day."

"I just never thought about it . . . for myself. Or for anybody else in our family, really. That's all. I don't think it's a bad thing. I just think to have a

56

boyfriend or girlfriend from a different race is really hard. I want to do the big sister thing and tell you to . . . I don't know. I don't want you to hurt, Ellie. That's all."

I stared down at my cuticle. It was bleeding now where I had chewed too deep. "That's what Marion told *you*, Anne," I said softly.

"I know. And I can't believe it's coming out of my mouth now. I can't believe I'm sitting here understanding how Marion felt."

"That's not right." I felt old suddenly. What had I expected—that she'd cry with happiness, that she'd come right home to meet him? No. Just that she'd . . . that she'd be there for this. The way she'd always been there.

"I gotta go," I said again.

"Listen, Ellie. I know you're pouting—"

"I'm not *pouting*. Don't do that, Anne."

"Do what?"

"Don't make it seem like I'm being a baby, okay."

"Okay," she said. "Look. I know it's New York, and I know things are different from when I was in high school and blah, blah, blah. But I have to be a big sister for a moment and say don't do something just 'cause you're mad at Marion or want to be radical—"

"You're such a jerk," I said. "When'd you get to be such a jerk?" I hung up before she could answer.

A long time ago, Anne used to talk about energy—how that was all love was—ions connecting across synapses of time and air. *Don't rationalize*, she'd say. *None of it will ever make sense.* I leaned back against the wall and closed my eyes, not wanting to cry. Anne was right. None of it made any sense.

Chapter
5

JEREMIAH SAT ON THE SIDELINES, EYEING THE GYM. IT was newer than Tech's—bigger. With fiberglass backboards, padded poles, and one of those floors that made you feel like you were bouncing when you jumped. In the center of it, a maroon and gray panther leaped over the Percy insignia. He watched Rayshon and Kennedy move with the rest of the team. Kennedy moved easily, the way he moved through the school. He was a junior and had been at Percy since his freshman year. He was friendly and popular. Rayshon was a sophomore. Mostly he kept to himself, sitting a bit away from the rest of the team during time-outs and leaving right after practice. His game was a little weak, but on the floor, he always smiled and slapped Miah five whenever one of them made a nice move. On their first day of practice, Rayshon had leaned over and whispered, "Just call us the three black musketeers." Jeremiah had smiled and nodded. It was a joke, but there was something deeper to it too. Something he and Rayshon and Kennedy understood.

"Move it or you'll be eating splinters for dinner, Joe," Coach Avery yelled to a freshman.

Jeremiah shook his head now, remembering his first practice. "You related to Norman Roselind—that filmmaker guy?" a kid named Braun had asked him.

"What you think we're all related?" Kennedy had said, smiling.

Braun looked embarrassed. They had been sitting on the bleachers waiting for the coach to show up. Jeremiah grabbed the ball from Kennedy and started dribbling. "Not related to anybody," he said, moving the ball back and forth between his legs. "Shoot! You think I'd be at this tired school if my daddy was a filmmaker?"

Everyone laughed. Braun slapped him five and

smiled. He liked Braun. And there were a couple of other cool guys on the team. But he missed Tech and Carlton and the homeboys he had played ball with since he was a little kid. He closed his eyes now. There was a picture of him and Carlton on his dresser. In the picture, they were both about eight, their arms around each other's shoulders, a basketball on the ground between them. A long time ago, he thought they'd always be playing ball together.

He scanned the team and sighed. These were his boys now—his team. And if he wanted to be part of the team, to make it work, he had to like them, had to respect them—no matter how weak their game was.

"Get your shirt off, Roselind," Coach said, pointing to the floor. "Joe, sit down."

Jeremiah lifted his sweatshirt over his head and jogged out onto the floor, slapping Joe's hand as they passed each other. He wasn't the tallest guy on the team, but in the week of practice, he had realized that he was easily the fastest and the best shot.

Kennedy passed him the ball and he took it down court, faked the guard, and took it up. It sank easily into the basket.

"Way to go, superstar," a sophomore named Peter whispered.

Jeremiah eyed him but didn't say anything.

"You got the moves, Ice, know what I'm saying?" Peter held his hand up for a high five. "My tag's Peter, Peter Hayle, remember? We kinda hung tight that first day."

"Yeah, sure," Jeremiah said, slapping Peter's hand. He hated when white guys tried to sound black.

"I got to learn to get my shot on like that. Get nice on the court like you do."

"It's all in the game," Jeremiah said.

They jogged down the court together. Rayshon looked over at them, shook his head, and smiled.

"Get my game on like you, I'll be like amped— know what I'm saying," Peter said, missing a pass.

"Get your head back in the game, Hayle," Coach called. "Concentrate!"

Jeremiah stole the ball, took it back down the court, and sunk it.

"What's this," Coach yelled, his face growing red. "A one-man team. Hit the showers! I'm through with you for the day." He picked up his clipboard and stormed out of the gym.

"Later," Rayshon said, slapping Jeremiah five. "You looked good out there today, man."

"Thanks," Jeremiah said, smiling.

Rayshon held his hand up for Peter to slap. "Later, lightskin."

Peter blushed. "I ain't lightskin, man," he said, slapping Rayshon's hand.

"I know." Rayshon grinned, winking at Jeremiah. He grabbed his bag, waved again, and headed out the gym.

"That homeboy's got a train to catch," Peter said. "I'd be stepping like that too, know what I'm saying?"

Jeremiah shook his head.

"Rayshon's paying his own way," Peter said, jogging beside him to the locker room. "Works two jobs. Last year, Percy finally hooked him up with a bit of cash but not the full ride."

Jeremiah pulled his T-shirt over his head, wiped the sweat off his neck with it, and opened his locker. "Must be some high-paying jobs," he said.

"My father hooked him up," Peter said. He ducked his head into the shower, ran water over it, then came back over to the bench and sat down, letting the water drip down his face. "My pops does a bit of advertising, know what I'm saying? Last year he hooked Rayshon up with a gig at his firm. Just like a trial thing, but Rayshon stepped to it and my pops was like, 'Man, I'm going keep this cat on.'"

"How come he doesn't have you working there?" Jeremiah asked.

Peter frowned at him. "I don't do the work thing. Gotta get my schooling on."

Jeremiah slammed his locker and headed toward the shower without saying anything. He hated that Rayshon had to run off to work and Peter got to sit here talking junk. Even if Peter's father *did* hook Rayshon up with a job, it didn't seem fair.

"You come 'round my way, we could get a nice game on," Peter said, smiling. "They got the fly courts over by me."

Jeremiah turned, feeling evil suddenly. "Why don't you come 'round *my* way?"

"Where you be crashing?" Peter asked, leaning against the locker. "I'm game."

"Fort Greene. Brooklyn."

Peter looked thoughtful for a moment. "Nah, man, I don't do Brooklyn. Strictly East Side ball is my game."

Jeremiah shook his head. "That's probably why it's so weak," he said, stepping into the shower stall and closing the door before Peter had a chance to answer.

He soaped up quickly then let the warm water run over his face and down his back for a few moments. In another stall, he could hear someone singing, loud and off-key. He bit his bottom lip. What was he doing here?

Change is a good thing, his grandma used to say. *Think of it like seasons. You don't want to stay one way all your life and have moss grow under your toes.*

He let the water run over him a few minutes longer. When he stepped out of the shower, Peter was gone. Jeremiah sighed, glancing at himself in the mirror. He was dark, dark and tall and wild haired. In the background, he could see his teammates moving around the locker room. He should have told them that first day who his father was. It would have sent them all packing. They thought he was just some regular guy from Brooklyn, but he wasn't. He was Norman Roselind's son. He was Nelia Roselind's son. He'd been all over the world.

Had probably seen places a lot of these guys couldn't even *spell*. Kennedy caught his eye and waved good-bye. Jeremiah watched him leave. Two black musketeers down, one to go.

What was he doing here with all these white boys around him?

He stared at the mirror, lost. That girl in the hall. "She's white too," he whispered, the words sinking in. He could hear someone laughing. It sounded like the whole world—pointing at him . . . and laughing.

Chapter
6

MONDAY MORNING, LIKE EVERY MORNING SINCE ANNE and I last talked, I stood in the kitchen with my hand on the phone. It was three hours earlier in San Francisco, but I knew Anne would be up. She had always risen at dawn, for as long as I could remember.

In the living room, I could hear Marion and Daddy talking softly.

This was stupid—all of it. I had only seen Jeremiah once since that first day—darting into a classroom, his hair bouncing behind him.

Jeremiah.

I tried to imagine us side by side. He was taller than me and skinny. Or at least he looked skinny with his pants hanging off of him. And his eyes. I had never seen eyes so light on a black person—almost green. Who'd he get them from? Who'd he get everything he had from? His dark smooth skin. His smile with the tiniest dimple right below his eye.

I swallowed. "Call me, Anne . . . *please*," I whispered. "Say the right thing." After a moment, I turned away from the phone, lifted my knapsack to my shoulders, and walked into the living room.

"I'm out of here," I said, waving.

My father glanced up from the *Times*. "No kisses?"

"No, not this morning," I said, slamming the door behind me.

At Seventy-Second Street, I cut through the park and bumped smack into a black guy. My stomach fluttered. He had locks and dark shades and reminded me of Jeremiah.

"Excuse me."

He nodded and kept going, a portfolio case bumping against his leg as he walked.

I turned and watched him, fingering the tiny Star

of David hanging from a gold chain around my neck. Why did I always bump into black guys? Was it something in the stars? I shook my head and smiled.

Once Anne and I were walking through Central Park when this black guy started running toward us. I frowned, remembering how Anne had screamed, and grabbed me. When the guy got up close, we realized he was a jogger, not a mugger or anything, and Anne had turned red with embarrassment.

I started walking again. Would Anne have reacted that way if the guy had been white? I put the Star of David in my mouth and sucked on it. It calmed me somehow, feeling it there.

I used to think it didn't matter—that everyone in this world had the same chance, the same fight. Imagine two babies born—one white, one black. Maybe their mothers shared the same hospital room and talked low—when all the excited visitors were gone and the hospital was heavy with sleep—about their futures. Talked about their dreams for the babies, long after the two A.M. feeding was over. I used to think that all those babies needed was some kind of chance—and a mother's dream for them. I was so . . . so silly back then. Naive. I *believed* stuff like that. Just because no one in this family had ever said a hateful thing about black people.

"All people," Marion was often saying. "All people have suffered. So why should any of us feel like we're better or less than another?"

But where were they then—these black people who were just like us—who were equal to us? Why weren't they coming over for dinner? Why weren't they playing golf with Daddy on Saturdays or quilting with Marion on Thursday nights? Why weren't they in our world, around us, a part of us?

Part Two

Chapter 7

IT RAINED AGAIN ON FRIDAY, A WARM, STEADY RAIN that turned the whole city gray. I sat in Mr. Hazelton's history class watching it. There was something sad about the rain. Marion had left on a rainy day. And Anne. The day she moved out it rained and rained. I turned back to my textbook. Jeremiah must have left Percy. It was already October and still I had only seen him once since that first day. That's what the rain made me feel now as it slammed against the windowpane—that I should stop hoping. People would always be leaving.

"I'd like all twenty-seven amendments memorized by—" Mr. Hazelton was saying.

"Excuse me."

I felt the room change. Felt the air around me grow warm suddenly—and still.

"I've been transferred over from Ms. Trousseau's class. My name is Jeremiah."

I lifted my head slowly, afraid I had heard wrong. He was standing there—in the front of the room— beautiful—the way I had remembered him.

Mr. Hazelton frowned as he studied Jeremiah's program card. "This late into the semester, Mr. Roselind?"

"Yes, sir." Jeremiah took a quick look around the room. His eyes flicked past me then back again. He smiled.

"Well, take a seat then," Mr. Hazelton said. "Look on with someone. You can pick up a textbook down in my office at the end of the day. You will memorize all twenty-seven amendments by Monday. Are you at all familiar with the amendments?"

"Yes, sir." Jeremiah looked annoyed.

"Good then. Take a seat."

He looked around the room again and nodded hello to a couple of people before walking slowly up the aisle toward me.

"Can I sit next to you?"

I nodded. He was taller than I had remembered and had pulled his hair back into a ponytail. When he sat down and smiled again, I smiled back. The smile felt shaky. Maybe my lips were trembling.

"Can I look on with you too?"

I nodded again, pressing my nails into my palms. My skin felt as though it would lift off.

"Can I have your book for keeps?"

I stared at him without saying anything, not sure what he was talking about. He grinned.

"I'm kidding."

"Oh."

"The right to privacy . . ." Mr. Hazelton was saying.

Jeremiah leaned over to look on with me. He smelled of musk and autumn—like he had just come in from outside. I stared down at the page and inhaled.

"Why'd you get transferred out of that other class?" I whispered.

"I knew it already. Remedial history. School made a *mistake*." He rolled his eyes.

"They do stuff like that all the time, I bet."

"Yeah—it just seems like more than a coincidence when it happens to me. Like what made them think I needed remedial anything. Nobody tested me. Nobody *asked* me. They just threw me in it then looked surprised when I knew it all. I mean, it makes you wonder—is it my *hair?*" He smiled.

I kind of half smiled, not sure what he was getting at.

"Or the melanin thing?"

The melanin thing. I played with the sentence a moment in my head and frowned. The world was like that a long time ago. But it wasn't like that anymore, was it? No. My stupid sister might be like that. And maybe my family sometimes. But not the rest of the world. Please not the rest of the world.

"Anyway," Jeremiah whispered, "I never got your name."

I swallowed. Mr. Hazelton was eyeing us. I turned to a clean page in my notebook and wrote "Ellie" across the top of it.

"Are you familiar with the fifth amendment, Mr. Roselind?"

"Yes, sir. The right to silence."

"Good. Maybe you and Elisha can take the fifth right now."

The class laughed and Jeremiah smiled. He had a beautiful smile.

"Yes, sir."

I stared at his hand resting on the textbook. His fingers were long and brown. Slowly, his hand moved across the textbook page and underneath my name. He ran his finger across it, then tapped it lightly and winked at me.

Chapter

8

SOME MORNINGS, IT SEEMED THE BELL WOULD NEVER ring, that he would never again walk to Mr. Hazelton's class and sit beside her. When it did ring, finally, he held tight to the straps of his knapsack as he walked, trying to keep from running there, running to the place where he could sit beside her. Ellie.

He found himself watching her when she wasn't looking. Watching the way she used her hand to move her hair out of her face, slowly, wrapping her fingers around it and pulling it back behind her ear. The way she leaned over her notebook to write, a tiny frown between her eyebrows. And her smile—she had a sweet smile. Sweet and sad and something else too. He couldn't explain it. If anyone asked, he wouldn't be able to put words to how he felt when Ellie looked at him and smiled. He felt something stop and start inside of him.

This afternoon, he had leaned across the desk and their shoulders touched. And Miah could feel the heat coming through her jacket. She had looked at him then and smiled. And they had stayed that way, with their shoulders touching, until the bell rang.

Jeremiah walked slowly now, his thumbs tucked into the straps of his knapsack. No one else at school had a leather one and now he understood why— one strap had already broken and he had had to stop at the shoe repair to get it sewn back on. And the books! He'd left two in his locker and stuffed the others into his bag as best as he could. Now the zipper was on its way to breaking. It was dumb—this leather knapsack was. First thing Saturday, he was going to go into the city, get a nylon one. Hers— Ellie's—was blue. He had seen her leaving school, had seen the way she clutched it to her chest as she walked—as though she was trying to hide something—

"Miah! Yo, Miah! Wait up!"

Jeremiah turned. Carlton was running toward him, dribbling a basketball, his curly brown hair blowing wild. Jeremiah lifted his backpack higher on his shoulder and stood there, watching Carlton head toward him. He had never really thought about it before—Carlton's white mama and black daddy. Had never even asked him what it was like. Ellie. Where did she live? Who were her parents?

"What's up?" Carlton grinned and chucked him the ball, then bent with his hands on his knees and took a few deep breaths. "I been calling your deaf behind for about three blocks now. That school got you thinking deep or something?"

"You just out of shape, man. Look at you, breathing all hard."

Carlton stood up and snatched the ball from him. "I ran from Atlantic and Fifth Avenue all the way over here to this piece of ground on South Portland in about seven minutes, so who's out of shape?"

"All I know is I'm not the one breathing like I just did some marathon."

He started walking again and Carlton fell in step beside him.

"Look at you all Percy'd out." Carlton grinned, eyeing Jeremiah's uniform.

Jeremiah looked down at himself. The burgundy jacket was made out of some kind of wool that itched around his neck and wrists. And the gray pants were cut strange. He had gotten them a size too big but that didn't make much difference. They still just sort of hung on him. When he had tried the uniform on at the end of the summer, his father had said he looked smart in it. But smart and good were two real different things and Jeremiah knew he didn't look his best on school days.

"I know. Ain't this some junk? I keep thinking I'm just going to walk in there and say the heck with it—kick it in some of my own clothes."

Carlton laughed.

"You walk up to that school dressed like Brooklyn, they'll send you packing. They'll be like, 'Oh no, we let a live one in here.' "

"You know it," Jeremiah said. "Least they let me pick my own shoes." He bent over and brushed an invisible speck of dust off of his hiking boots. They were black and lug soled.

"Those are some sweet boots," Carlton said. "But give me my own clothes any day."

Jeremiah nodded. Carlton was wearing a pair of jeans and a green sweatshirt with *Wisdom* stitched across the front. He dribbled the ball easily back and forth through his legs as they walked.

"Tech miss me?"

"Nah—not really. They probably won't even notice you're gone until the season starts." Carlton laughed. "Anything happening over at Percy?"

"Nah," Jeremiah said, shaking his head. "They're some kind of raggedy. Took third last year. I'm scared to see who we're up against. Must be a couple of nursing homes thrown in there."

Carlton smiled. "They must think they got a piece of heaven with you." He raised the ball above Jeremiah's head. "Mr. Twenty-two points a game."

"And that was on a bad day," Jeremiah added.

"Let's not get crazy, Miah. I remember a couple of no-pointer games—donut, zero, circles, hula hoop—score nothing—games." He laughed. His eyes lit up when he laughed in a way that made his whole face seem brighter.

Jeremiah smiled.

"I must have been injured."

"Your *game* was injured but *you* were fine."

They walked along without saying anything for a while. Jeremiah watched Carlton take the ball up on his finger and spin it. He was a year older than Jeremiah and a starting forward at Tech. Their coach had said Carlton was one of the best players Tech had ever seen.

"You want to get out of that buffalo soldier's uniform and shoot some?" Carlton tossed the ball against a building, jumped high, and caught it. He started singing the Bob Marley song about the guy being stolen from Africa to fight against Africa in America.

"Oh, is that what it is?" Jeremiah laughed. "So I'm gonna be shipped back to my own homeland to fight, huh?"

Carlton threw him the ball. "Yep."

They were at his mother's stoop. Jeremiah looked over at his father's window knowing he'd have to sleep there tonight. It'd been a week since he'd stayed with him. He sighed and sat on the bottom stair. "Well, which is the enemy's homeland and which one is my own?"

Carlton stopped dribbling and ran his fingers through his hair. "Your daddy still shacking up with Lois Ann?"

Jeremiah nodded.

"Yeah. And Mama's still mad as all get out about it all." He pulled his knapsack off his shoulders and stared up at the sky. It was beautiful today, all warm and gold. The leaves had begun to change, and the trees up and down the block cast pretty shadows over everything. He loved October. Had always loved it. There was something sad and beautiful about it—the ending and beginning of things.

"That's rough, Miah."

Carlton sat down beside him.

"I mean, they didn't really get along all that well—like in front of the cameras they did, but not in private. Not even in front of me. They'd go days without speaking and everything would feel all tight and hot . . ." He frowned and stared at his hands. "I wouldn't even want to come home some days. . . . But it was still something—they still had something. It was raggedy but it was something."

"Yeah, I feel you," Carlton said. "But when my parents start arguing I'm like, 'Just break up already and give us all a break.' "

"How come they don't?"

Carlton shrugged. "I think they know there's nobody else in the whole world who would live with either of them. Even my sister—she graduated high school and jetted all the way to *England* to go to college. I feel like telling them, 'Listen, you know something's up if your only daughter went all the way to England to get away from you.' "

They laughed. Across the street two little girls sat on a stoop playing jacks. Further down the block somebody was playing a Stevie Wonder tune on the piano. The music drifted slowly past them.

"I figure I might go to Zimbabwe or somewhere. Two years I'll be eighteen and done with school and on my way."

Jeremiah nodded. "Zimbabwe, huh?"

"Yeah. My daddy doesn't like the heat. And Mama got sick last time she went to Africa. Figure they wouldn't follow me there."

Jeremiah smiled and shook his head. "You crazy, man."

"Yeah, I'm crazy—but at least I'll be crazy and far away."

He started singing softly—a song about being somewhere on the other side of the ocean. It was a pretty song—sad and quiet. Jeremiah rested his head against the banister and listened. Carlton had a good voice. His father was a musician, and some nights Jeremiah would walk by their building and he'd hear the two of them harmonizing. Those nights, his heart felt like it was closing up inside his chest and he missed his own father so much it hurt.

"Carlton . . ." he said softly now.

Carlton stopped singing and rubbed the back of his hand across his eyes. He was quiet for a moment and Jeremiah looked away from him, embarrassed suddenly. He wondered if Carlton had been crying.

"Yo," Carlton said after a few moments had passed. "What's up?"

"What's it like, man—to have a white mama and a black daddy?"

"You have a black daddy."

"I know. I want to know about the other part though—what's that like?"

Carlton shrugged and stared straight ahead. "I don't know. I mean, I don't know any other way. My dad's a good man. My moms is a good woman. It's weird sometimes—you know—like when we go out west to visit her family. They're so . . . so stiff around us—they're not like my mama. You know how she is—she's cool. I don't feel like they're my people—I never really did even though I know they are. . . . And sometimes people stare when me and my moms and dad are together, like they're trying to figure it all out or something. Black people and white people. And sometimes they kind of look at us like, 'Oh, I get it—it's an interracial thing.' You know. Like that. I think Colette went to England to get away from it all."

Jeremiah nodded. He had had a crush on Carlton's sister. When they were younger he used to try to tease her just to get her to smile. Sometimes she'd tickle him until he thought he'd pass out. And he would scream, begging her to stop, wanting her to stop but hoping she wouldn't. Colette always smacked them gently on the head before leaving them alone. Jeremiah touched the side of his head now. That was years ago, but whenever he thought about it, he could feel the imprint of her hand.

"I'm going to jet out there next summer," Carlton was saying. "I miss her. I mean she was a pain sometimes, but when you only have one sister, you learn to let them be a pain sometimes and just ignore that part of their personality. . . ."

His voice drifted off.

"I wouldn't know."

"Yeah—it's kind of crazy, don't you think? You sitting up in that big house an only child. Your parents could have filled it with four or five kids and still had room to throw a party if they wanted to."

"Could of. Yo, Carl—I need to speak with you about something."

Carl looked at him without saying anything.

"I met this girl at school—this white girl."

"Yeah—and . . ."

"I don't know. I just never really thought about that—about dating a white girl."

Carlton smiled. "What makes you think she's thought about dating *you?*"

"I don't know." He looked up at his father's window. "Sometimes I feel like I don't know *nothing* about *nothing.*"

"Yeah."

"I mean—me and that girl—her name's Ellie—we barely said anything to each other. But it's strange . . ." He looked at Carlton. "It's like I know her—like I can look inside her and see everything. I know it sounds craz—"

"You sound like you're in love, man."

Jeremiah frowned. "Nah. I don't even know her." But he remembered that first day, bending with her to pick up her books in the hallway. Something inside him went cold that morning—cold and hot all at once. "I couldn't even tell you her last name." He was thoughtful for a moment. "But I was sitting next to her in class today—and I don't know—I felt like we . . . like we should always be next to each other. I don't know."

Carlton stood up and tucked the ball under his arm. "Sounds like love, man."

"But she's *white*."

Carlton raised an eyebrow. "Hello, Miah. Look who you talking to, man. It happens. And you know what? It ain't the worst thing in the world."

Chapter 9

THE APARTMENT WAS EMPTY AND STILL. I STOOD AT THE foot of the stairway watching the yellow-gold sunlight stream in from the living room window, and listening to the messages on the answering machine. My father had called from the hospital to say hello. Marc had called and the twins. And Susan—my older sister who was a therapist in Santa Cruz. She was more like an aunt than a sister—older and distant the way grown-ups can be. I pressed the "save" button and sat down on the bottom stair, leaning my head against the banister.

Anne was different. Even though she's ten years older, she acted silly sometimes. I missed that Anne—the one that laughed so hard, whatever she was drinking came out of her nose. The Anne who had taken me on the Staten Island ferry when I was ten and surprised me with a cooler full of vendor hotdogs—all done up with onions and sauerkraut and mustard the way I loved them.

I closed my eyes now, remembering how me and Anne sat devouring hotdogs and watching the city grow smaller behind us as the ship pulled away from it.

Where was that Anne now? Marion had spoken to her a couple of times, but she never asked for me, the way she always used to. I pressed my forehead against the banister and swallowed. What had I done that was so wrong?

I heard Marion's key in the door and got up, not wanting her to see me sitting like this.

"Marion . . . ?" I called, heading into the kitchen.

My father was standing at the refrigerator, pulling out sandwich meat and mayonnaise.

"No—not Marion—Edward—Dad to you. Why do you torture your mother like that, Ellie?" my father asked, his eyes twinkling. They were gray-blue like Anne and Ruben's.

I kissed him on the cheek. "That's why. Because *you* call me Ellie and she calls me Elisha."

He sliced some bread from a loaf Marion had baked a few days before and started piling turkey onto it.

"I feel like I haven't seen you in forever."

My father nodded. He looked tired and thin in his blue shirt and khakis, his stethoscope dangling from his pocket. His hair was like mine, but the curls were gray now and starting to thin.

"In the emergency room this week. All week. Wouldn't be surprised if they had to throw *me* up on a table."

"You shouldn't work so hard, Daddy." I poured a glass of juice and set it on the table then put his sandwich on a plate. "I missed you this Sunday."

We used to spend Sunday afternoons together, sitting and reading the *New York Times*. In the middle of an article, my father would frown and press his thumb against a paragraph. "Listen to this crazy thing that's happening, Ellie," he'd say, then slowly read, overemphasizing paragraphs he thought outrageous. And I'd lean back against the fireplace wall—I always sat on the floor those afternoons—with my ankles crossed, my eyes closed in concentration.

"Sunday afternoon," my father said, smiling,

"this intern came in carrying the *Times* and I thought—I'm not going to read it until I can read it with my Ellie."

"You didn't even glance at it?"

He shook his head solemnly. "Didn't even see what books were being reviewed. But this Sunday—back to the olden days." He laughed, sat down at the table across from me, and took a bite of his sandwich.

I leaned on my hand, watching him. It's hard to remember when the ritual of reading the *Times* with my father began. When I was small I remember sitting on the floor, listening to him read. Of course, Marion disapproved. Every Sunday, as she fussed about the kitchen preparing dinner, she'd punctuate our quiet time with complaints. *Elisha should be out—with friends her own age. Go to a museum. Go to a movie. Get off your rump. You're becoming an old man.* And my father would wink at me. *And what's wrong with becoming an old man?* he'd called to Marion, who'd make annoyed noises and say, *Don't be ridiculous.*

He lifted his glasses now, rubbed his eyes, and smiled.

I got up, poured myself a glass of orange juice, and sat back down across from him.

"So tell me about this boy Marion says you met at Percy."

I frowned and didn't say anything.

"Oh—don't go getting upset, Ellie. Your mother just mentioned it in passing—that you had met someone you liked. Anne told her."

"What else did Anne say?"

My father shrugged. "Nothing. She said to ask you. What would *you* say?"

"Nothing. There isn't a boy, Daddy. Just this guy I met who—nothing." Where would I begin anyway? In the same place I tried to begin with stupid Anne?

"Are we going to get to meet this, this nothing?"

My father was smiling, but I didn't feel like smiling back.

I reached across the table and picked a piece of turkey out of what was left of his sandwich.

"His name is Jeremiah," I said slowly. "I don't remember his last name. Rosedale or something. On the first day of school I dropped my books and then he helped me pick them up and then I don't know. Now he's in my history class."

"Is he nice?"

I shrugged. "We didn't really talk a whole lot, but

94

he seems nice. And Mr. Hazelton wants us to re-member all twenty-seven amendments by Friday. Jeremiah says he knows them already. In order."

My father whistled, impressed. "Do you know what his parents do?"

I took a swallow of orange juice. "Don't care."

He smiled. "And why should you?" He finished his sandwich and pushed the plate away. "Well, he sounds nice enough. And if he's smart I don't see any reason why you couldn't be friends."

"I didn't know you and Marion were looking for reasons." I felt myself getting mad again.

"Not reasons—excuses, I guess. We don't want our baby leaving the nest just yet. It makes us feel old." He stood up, reached over and touched my cheek. "It reminds us that one day this house will be empty—no children, just two ancient people padding through it looking at pictures."

"I'm not going anywhere just yet, Daddy. You got a whole' nother three years of me."

"Three years isn't a long time, Ellie. You'll see."

I sat at the kitchen table long after my father had gone upstairs to take a nap. Something about what he had said depressed me. Yes, of course I'd leave the way my sisters and brothers had. But that did seem like a long time away. Each day seemed to crawl slowly into the next and the next, and some nights I couldn't sleep with the excitement of a new day—and another chance to see Jeremiah. Maybe this was what love felt like. I turned the empty orange juice glass around and around in my hand. Was it lying that I didn't tell him Jeremiah was black? Why should that matter? Why did any of it matter?

Outside, the sun was setting over Central Park. I pressed my hand to my lips—wondering what it would feel like to kiss Jeremiah. Wondering if I'd always be wondering.

Chapter

10

IN THE LATE AFTERNOON SUNLIGHT, JEREMIAH STOOD IN his mother's room, running his hands over her dresser, softly fingering the bottles of lotion and the pictures in silver frames—him at two in a diaper and T-shirt, pointing at her, her smiling into the camera, the two of them walking in a park somewhere—maybe he was five in that one. And then at the far end of her dresser, in a tiny frame, a picture of her in a wedding dress, holding a bouquet of white roses. Jeremiah picked it up and stared at it. His mother was smiling and looking off, away from the camera. Maybe to where his father stood. His father. Jeremiah bit down on his bottom lip. Where was he right now? With Lois Ann somewhere. Once he had run into them in Manhattan—his father and Lois Ann, walking slowly down Spring Street, his father's arm around Lois Ann's shoulder. And for a moment, as he walked toward them, Jeremiah had thought Lois Ann was his mother and he had smiled. And his father had smiled back, cautiously, slowly, like he couldn't believe what he was seeing—his son walking toward him, smiling.

How long had it been since Jeremiah had smiled in the presence of the two of them. Months maybe. He had smiled that first day, years and years ago, when he didn't know anything—before the news of his father's affair got out. He had come home to find his father sitting with Lois Ann on their stoop, and he had smiled. Smiled because it was so rare to find his father home relaxing, a glass of wine in one hand and a copy of a video in the other. "I been waiting for you to get home from school," his father had said. "Figured we could watch this movie together." And Jeremiah had smiled even wider— because he was young then, maybe twelve or thirteen, and he didn't know the ways people—his parents—could hurt each other. Yeah—he was only twelve or thirteen, and he didn't know that Lois Ann and his father had a thing going on, a heavy thing that would eventually break the family apart.

Jeremiah squinted at the picture now. He could feel tears coming on, a thick knot of them rising up in the back of his throat. It had to do with this picture of his mother in her wedding dress and October and the lazy afternoon sun streaming through the window. It had to do with Ellie and Percy Academy and the fact that maybe he was a little bit in love with a white girl he barely knew. But mostly—right now, standing in his mama's room holding this picture close, it had to do with them, his parents.

They had married in Prospect Park—in the boathouse—on an amazingly blue day in October. It would be seventeen years tomorrow. Seventeen years ago, they had thought they'd be together forever—and in some ways, seventeen years *is* forever. Eleven movies in seventeen years. Three books—and maybe his mother would have written more if she hadn't had him. And maybe that's why they never had another one. But the only child thing—that had stopped mattering so much a long time ago. Yeah, sometimes he wanted a brother or sister, but it was more than that. He wanted more than that too—somebody deep. Somebody who could know him—know all of him—the crazy things he dreamed on stormy nights, when he woke with tears in his eyes and pulled the covers tight around him. How alone he felt most days—even with his homeboys surrounding him—the way the loneliness settled deep inside of him and lingered.

He placed the picture back on the shelf gently and closed his eyes. Ellie was there—behind his eyelids, smiling at him. What would become of them? Today in class, he had caught her staring at him, a tiny smile on her lips. Jeremiah stared back without smiling. He couldn't smile. There was something scary about the way he felt—light-headed and out of control. The whole classroom seemed to drop away, and for a minute, it seemed like it was only the two of them in the world. Then Mr. Hazelton said something and the class faded back around them. Jeremiah turned back to his textbook. When Mr. Hazelton called on him, he stuttered some answer that seemed to satisfy the teacher. But he wasn't in that room anymore. He was somewhere far away. With Ellie.

I'm going to kiss you soon, Jeremiah had found himself thinking. *I don't know when or where or how, but soon I'm going to kiss you.*

And later, as he changed into his gym clothes, he had found himself thinking about her, imagining the two of them together somewhere. Somewhere.

He needed someone to talk to. Someone who knew him well enough to rub his head and say, "Everything's going to be all right." There was something like a fire in his chest, something hot and tight and unfamiliar.

Jeremiah felt the emptiness of the house settle down around him. Where was his mother? Where had all the people who used to fill these rooms gone to?

"Daddy . . . " he whispered. "Mama . . ."

The house echoed. Jeremiah sat down on the edge of his mama's bed, pulled his knees up to his chin, and wrapped his arms around them.

And with the late afternoon light casting heavy shadows across everything, Jeremiah rested his head against his legs. And cried.

Chapter
11

"JEREMIAH."

I had been walking the halls when I found him standing alone, his head pressed against a window.

"Hey, Ellie," he said, turning away from the window. "That's funny. I was just thinking . . . about . . . about you."

I looked down at my shoes, embarrassed suddenly. "What were you thinking?"

"I don't know. You were passing through my mind—just kind of floating through it."

He had been thinking about me. I had been floating through his mind. All morning I'd been imagining this moment, meeting Jeremiah in the hall. But I hadn't thought it would happen, that I'd turn a corner and find him standing here, his head pressed against the window, his locks falling softly around his shoulders, thinking about *me*. No one had ever just been thinking about me. It felt odd— good odd, the idea that I was on someone's mind. On Jeremiah's mind.

"People call me Miah," he said softly. He had the most beautiful smile.

The hall was empty, quiet and dim. In the distance, I could hear a teacher talking. His voice was muffled, like it was coming from behind a closed door. The late bell had rung a long time ago.

"Miah. I like that. What's your last name?"

We were whispering now, but in the empty hallway, our words seemed loud.

Miah turned back to the window. After a moment he said, "Roselind," so softly, I could barely hear him.

"Jeremiah Roselind. That's pretty. Really pretty."

Miah shrugged. "It's just a name. What's yours— your last name?"

"Eisen. Elisha Sidney Eisen. My parents went to Australia and liked it—I think they thought it was clever to name me after a city."

Miah smiled. "Elisha. Ellie. I like both names."

"I like Ellie better."

"Then I like Ellie better too. You don't have class this period, Ellie?"

I shook my head. "Trig. I'm not going. How about you?"

"English. I know it already. They're reading *Catcher in the Rye.* I read that book three times already. Figure I'll go back when the rest of the class catches up."

We stood staring at each other, my heart beating hard beneath my Percy shirt. I folded my arms across my chest wanting to quiet it. Afraid he'd be able to hear it and laugh. Jeremiah turned back to the window.

"You ever get scared, Ellie?"

I swallowed, embarrassed. "Yeah." It was not supposed to be like this—this real, this close to who I was. Like he could look right through me.

"Like right now?"

"Yeah."

He turned back to me. "I could see it. In your eyes. How scared you are. You've got the kind of eyes that don't hide anything."

I felt my face getting red.

"People used to say I had eyes like that," he said softly. "But I learned how to work them. To hide stuff."

"You think that's better?"

A tall skinny boy turned the corner, giving us a look as he passed. Miah stared back and the guy kind of waved and kept walking.

"I don't know what's better," Miah said. "What's gonna happen is gonna happen. I mean, the feeling's still there even if you're covering it up. You feel like walking? Getting out of here for a bit?"

"What's the penalty for cutting?" I asked, even though I knew I'd follow him—anywhere. When Anne used to talk about being in love, she said it felt like someone wrapping you inside of them. And that's what I felt like now, like slowly I was being wrapped inside of Miah—inside his eyes, inside his voice, inside the way he talked about things.

Miah smiled. "I don't know. Never did it before."

"Me either," I said, relieved. I had been afraid he was a cutter, and if he was, I'd probably like him less. I didn't want to like him less.

He lifted his knapsack onto his shoulder. "You live in Manhattan?"

I nodded and bent to pull up one of the stupid knee socks Percy made girls wear.

"Then I'm following you."

It had rained all morning. Now the sun was out again, warm and bright. Miah pulled off his jacket and stuffed it across his knapsack straps so that it hung down behind him. We crossed Fifth Avenue and headed into Central Park.

Two old women, walking arm in arm, eyed us. Jeremiah frowned, glaring at them.

"Are you all right?" one of the women asked me. I nodded.

"Biddies," Jeremiah said under his breath. He started walking faster.

"They asked that 'cause you're with me, you know," he said, eyeing me. He looked hurt and angry all at once. "If you were with a white boy, they probably would have just smiled and kept on going."

I moved closer to him. "They're just sheltered Upper East Siders," I said. "And old."

"Yeah," Miah said. I could tell he didn't believe me.

"It's not anything. Just two old stupid women."

Jeremiah looked at me for a moment then looked away. I could see his jawbone moving beneath his skin. He knew what I knew. That it was something more than stupid old women. And that I'd try to make it into nothing, to make it less embarrassing for them. For us.

We walked a while without saying anything. I felt hot suddenly, clammy. Clammy and white. White and clammy. Why hadn't I said anything to those stupid women. *Yes, I'm okay*, I should have said. And maybe, maybe if I was brave I would've taken Miah's hand.

"If my dad knew I was cutting, he'd hit the roof," Jeremiah said. "He'd say that school is too expensive to even be missing even a *half* of a class."

"Do your parents complain about it?" I asked, my voice coming slow and shaky. We were walking along a cobblestone path, and I tried to let the old women slip from my mind. But they were there, their pinched faces scowling at us.

Miah glanced at me, then looked away and shook his head. "My dad pays. He doesn't say much as long as he knows I'm going every day. Just asks how it's going and blasé blasé. They separated—my parents did. Whatever."

"That's too bad. I mean—I guess it's too bad, right?"

He shrugged. "It's whatever. Your parents together?"

I nodded, embarrassed. At Jefferson, there were only a few of us whose parents hadn't divorced yet. "They'll be together forever. No one else could take either of them."

"Oh—it's that kind of gig?"

"Yeah."

"I guess that's cool."

"I guess. I mean—my father is—my father's great. You like your dad?"

"Sometimes," he said, frowning.

"Here is good," I said, stopping at a wide patch of grass underneath a maple tree.

The air around us seemed thick suddenly, hot and stifling. When I looked over at Miah, he was still frowning.

"Yeah," Miah said. "This is cool. You want to sit on my jacket?"

I shook my head and spread my own jacket beneath me.

Miah sat down next to me, so close I could see the tiny hairs growing above his top lip. They were very black—like his hair—and fine. It felt strange having him so close to me. Strange in a good way.

He unzipped his knapsack and started rummaging through it. After a moment, he came up with a Snickers bar. He searched through it some more and came up with a Swiss Army knife and cut the Snickers bar down the middle, handed half to me and put the knife back in his knapsack.

"Thanks, Miah," I said, really meaning it. I pulled the wrapping away and took a small bite. The chocolate was starting to melt already. It tasted sweet and warm.

"My father gave me that knife. He said we'd go camping soon. That was about four years ago and we haven't gone camping yet. But I carry that knife everywhere." He smiled and looked at me. "Never know when he's gonna pop up and say, 'Hey, Miah—let's take that camping trip we been talking about.' "

"You think he ever will?"

Miah shook his head. "No. I'm too old now. And everything's changed since he gave it to me. I guess I just hold on to it."

"Hoping."

"Yeah," he said. "Hoping."

"When I was little ..." I said slowly. My voice felt shaky. "Marion used to leave us. We'd wake up and she'd be gone." It felt strange hearing myself say this to Miah—hearing that she left us.

"Who's Marion?"

"My mother." I pulled my hair out of my face and smiled. "I call her that. She hates it, but she won't call me Ellie so I call her Marion."

Miah nodded without taking his eyes away from mine. He looked older when he was listening, grown-up and serious.

"I didn't think she was ever coming back."

"Did she?"

"Yeah. Both times. But after the second time, it was different. I was the only kid still living at home and I was scared around her—careful. After a couple of months, things kind of went back to normal. But I don't think it was ever the same again. It was like ... like she had *introduced* this idea of leaving to me and I'd never even thought about it before."

I ate my half of the Snickers bar slowly, thinking about the day Marion returned. It had snowed that morning—a heavy wet snow. My father helped me into my coat and hat and our neighbor came to take me to the park. We built a snowman. It was the first time I'd ever built one. When I got home, wet and cold and ready for my father to make me some hot chocolate, Marion was sitting there, at the kitchen table, her hands folded like a schoolgirl. I stared at her a long time waiting for her to hug me, to start bawling and talking about how much she missed me. But when she reached out her arms, it was me who started bawling.

"We never thought she'd leave," I said again. "And after she came back, I never believed she'd stay."

"You believe it now?" Miah asked.

"I don't think I care so much anymore." I folded the empty Snickers wrapper over and over itself. "I survived the first time. It makes me know I can always survive. But there's this other part of me that doesn't believe anyone's ever going to stay. Anywhere."

"Wonder why she came back." Miah said.

I looked up into the leaves and squinted, liking the way the green twisted and blurred in the sunlight. I felt lighter somehow. Free. "I asked her. She said it was because our family was all she knew—all she had. Squint like this, Miah. And see what it does to the leaves."

Miah looked up and squinted, then smiled. "Feels like I'm spinning," he said softly. "Or like the whole world is spinning and I'm the only thing on it that's not moving."

I felt his hand closing over mine and swallowed. It felt warm and soft and good.

I closed my eyes, wanting to stay this way always, with the sun warm against my face and Miah's hand on mine.

"There's this poem," he said, "that my moms used to read to me. 'If you come as softly/as the wind within the trees./You may hear what I hear./See what sorrow sees./If you come as lightly/as threading dew,/I will take you gladly,/nor ask more of you.'/When you told me that thing about Marion, it made me think of it. The way stuff and people come and go."

"It's pretty, that poem." I closed my eyes. Maybe people were always coming toward each other— from the beginning of their lives. Maybe Miah had always been coming toward me, to this moment, sitting in Central Park holding hands. Coming softly.

"You ever wish you were small again, Ellie? That there was somebody still tucking you in and reading you stories and poetry?"

I turned my hand over and laced my fingers in his. His hand was so soft and warm. Above us, the leaves fluttered, strips of sun streaming gold down through them. I swallowed.

"All the time," I whispered.

"Me too. You gonna let me kiss you, Ellie?"

I nodded, feeling my stomach rise and dip, rise and dip, until Miah's lips were on mine, soft and warm as his hand.

Then everything grew quiet and still and perfect.

Chapter
12

His father's light was on. Miah climbed the stairs slowly and unlocked the outside door. He looked over his shoulder at his mother's window. Dark. He wondered if she was out or sitting alone in the darkness.

"That you, Miah-man?" his father called.

"Yeah."

"Come on into the living room and meet some people."

Miah frowned. He didn't want to meet some people. He wanted to go up to his room, lie on his bed, and think about Ellie. About today in the park. About the way her lips felt against his. Different.

The same. Right. And his hand over hers—the brown and the white, her tiny fingers, the silver band on her thumb, her eyes, the way they just kept on looking and looking deeper and deeper inside of him. No one had ever looked at him like that, like they wanted to know every single thing about him. Like everything he had to say mattered. Really mattered.

"Miah . . . ?"

"Be right there," he said, taking off his jacket and loosening his tie. He could hear voices and laughter—Lois's laughter rising up higher than everyone else's. It had always been like this—the house full of people. When his mother and father were still together, he had liked it. But heading into the room now, he realized again how rarely he got to be alone with his father for more than a short time.

"This my boy I talk so much about." His father grinned. He was sitting in an overstuffed chair, a beer on the table beside him. Lois was leaning on the chair behind him, her arms draped around his shoulders. She was pretty—with curly hair and clear red brown skin. Not as pretty as his mama but pretty enough to turn heads. His father looked good this evening, relaxed and smiling, his long legs propped up on an ottoman.

Two couples sat on the couch smiling and looking like they had been there a while. Miah mumbled hellos to them, leaned forward to shake everyone's hand the way he had done since he was three.

"Oh, my lord, Norman, this child is *beautiful*," one of the women said, an older plump woman with short locks. "Where'd you adopt him?"

They laughed. Miah smiled but didn't say anything. He knew he looked a lot like his dad but mostly like his mother. His dad was tall and brown with jet-black hair that had begun to recede and a wide opened smile.

"How old are you? Twenty-five?" the woman teased.

"Fifteen," Miah said. He grinned. It always made him feel good when older women flirted with him.

"Well, I can wait," she said.

"You better wait until I die," the man sitting beside her said. " 'Cause *no one* is going *nowhere* until I do."

They laughed again.

"Sit down, Miah," his father said. "Get yourself a soda or something."

"Ahm—I have a lot of homework."

"Percy working you?"

He nodded to his father. "They're trying to. I think I have it under control."

"You eat anything yet?" Lois Ann asked. "I can make you something right fast."

"Thanks. I got a slice of pizza after practice. I'm okay."

"Well, you go get your work on then," his father said. "I'll be up later on to say good night."

"You still getting tucked in?" the heavy woman asked.

Miah smiled but didn't say anything. "It was nice meeting you all."

"See you when you're twenty-five," the woman said.

Upstairs, alone in his room, Jeremiah lay back on his bed and stared up at the ceiling. *I kissed her. I kissed Ellie. Elisha Sidney Eisen.* He wanted to scream, to run to his window, throw it open and yell it to the world. *Right there in Central Park with the sun coming through the leaves and everything around all right. Everything all right.*

Outside the sun was beginning to set. He wanted

to tell somebody—not the way he and his home-boys talked, bragging about which girl they'd been with, giving all the details, lying mostly, and slapping each other five over it. No. Not like that. He wanted to sit with his head bent toward somebody, whispering—how strange and perfect it all was. How . . . how *precise* and brilliant. Yeah, those were the words he'd use if someone was there. If someone was listening.

Miah sighed and turned toward the window. He could hear his father and Lois Ann laughing with their friends. He could hear girls outside chanting, *Ten, twenty, thirty, forty, one, ten, twenty, thirty, forty, two.* And in the distance, he heard the vague sound of a basketball, someone bouncing it slowly, some young kid somewhere, learning how to handle the ball, how to keep it near him. How to keep control.

He remembered those early days—the ball feeling big and unmanageable in his little hands. He remembered trying to dribble with two hands and the big boys saying, *Nah, Little Miah—you got to handle it. You got to use one hand. Make the ball yours. Show it who's the boss.* And the first time he felt a leather ball leave his hands and sail into the basket—a leather ball his father had given him for his ninth birthday. How different it felt from the vinyl ones he had always known. *Don't use this playing ball in the park,* his father had warned. But, of course, he had taken it to the park and played game after game there until the ball was ragged and dead.

And he remembered being older, running along the sidewalk, feeling like he was flying, and the ball, a vinyl one again, right there beside him, flying beside him like they were connected by some invisible string.

Last Sunday, he had helped Little Ray from down the block dribble, helped him wrap his tiny six-year-old hands around the ball, stood behind him as he lifted it toward the basket and missed. *You gotta want it to go in, Little Ray,* he'd said. *You got to believe it can.* And they had practiced shot after shot until finally, late in the afternoon, the ball sailed in smoothly, without touching the backboard or the rim. Swish. And Little Ray had grinned, jumped up and down, and slapped Miah five. *Yeah,* Miah had said. *I know the feeling.*

Chapter

13

A WEEK PASSED. AND THEN ANOTHER. AND SUDDENLY it was cold and the whole city seemed to be wrapped in a thin layer of wind and rain.

Early Saturday morning, Susan called to apologize again for not making it home for Yom Kippur. I sat at the top of the stairs, listening to Marion give her a hard time. "Not one of my kids showed up," she said.

Marion was an expert at the guilt thing. "Don't forget to tell her that you and Daddy and the kid that is still stuck here didn't do anything for Yom Kippur. Make sure you tell her we broke the fast at Wendy's—and that you had a *cheeseburger.*"

Marion put her finger to her lips and scowled at me.

"If I told her that," she said, after she'd hung up, "she'd find a way not to show up for Hanukkah either. You want to spend that holiday too with just me and your father?"

I shook my head.

"Anyway, Anne called while you were in the shower," Marion said. "She said give her a call as soon as you can."

"What else did she say?" We hadn't spoke since the afternoon I told her about Jeremiah.

Marion gave me a puzzled look. "To call her— what—do you think she's going to tell *me* what it's about. Does anyone tell me anything about anything."

I smiled, tucked my hair behind my ear, and headed back toward my room. "The rumor is you have a big mouth, Marion."

"As if I care about commitment ceremonies and boys . . ." Marion called.

I turned and glared at her. I hated Anne. "What exactly did she tell you?"

Marion shrugged. "That you two had fallen out

over a boy. And I'm guessing it's not because you like the same one either—since boys aren't exactly Anne's type." She looked at me a moment, then grew serious. "You can talk to me too, you know . . . Ellie. We can be close if you want. We can talk about things."

I sighed and sat down on the stairs again. How could I tell her it was too late to start growing close—that we had lost that chance years and years ago?

"There's nothing to talk about . . . Ma," I said softly. "When there is, I promise, I'll talk to you."

Marion nodded, turned to the sink, and began washing breakfast dishes. She tucked one foot behind the other in a way that made my eyes fill up. She looked broken. Defeated. Lonely.

Chapter 14

No one at Percy said anything. It was strange the way the students seemed to turn away from it, from him and Ellie holding hands on the Percy stairs. From his arm around Ellie's shoulder as they walked through the halls. Turn away from them kissing outside their classrooms. Sometimes Miah imagined their turning away in slow motion—the eyes cast downward, the heads moving slowly above the collars of Percy uniforms.

Yeah, they looked, and once, Miah had caught two black girls staring at him and Ellie and whispering. When he looked up, the girls turned away. They didn't seem angry or surprised or hurt. Nothing like that. Just two girls talking—saying something about him and Ellie, then getting caught. And, slowly, turning away.

Even Braun. Even Rayshon and Kennedy. Some days Miah thought he'd ask them—try to get it going the way he used to do with his homeboys. Maybe mention the afternoons they spent in Central Park. Get them all talking about the girls they'd been with and see what happened when he got around to *really* talking about Ellie. Would they turn away then? Ask what it was like with her? Maybe Kennedy or Rayshon would ask if it was different with white girls. Or Joe and Braun would wonder about the black girls at school. Maybe all of them already knew.

"Can I take your picture?" a kid asked one morning.

They had been sitting on the stairs, waiting for the bell to ring. There were other Percy kids around them, talking and looking over notes. Two boys were doing tricks on skateboards, jumping over the fire hydrant and twirling on two wheels.

Miah looked at Ellie. When she nodded, he nodded too, and the camera flashed on them.

Then the kid with the camera was gone. And the students around them were gathering their books together and heading inside. First period bell rang and the kids with the skateboards rushed past them, their boards jammed under their arms. Someone said hi to Ellie. A guy from the team tapped Miah on the head as he passed him.

The morning moved on as if this moment, the moment of him and Ellie, had always been here.

And always would be.

Chapter
15

WHEN I WAS LITTLE, ANNE USED TO TALK TO ME ALL the time about love. She said sometimes it happened slowly, an investment of work and time over months and years. She said that kind of love was sort of like the stock market—that, little by little, you put all of yourself into it and hoped for a decent return. She said there were other kinds too— the quick-fix binge love—when a person bounced from person to person without taking a bit of time out to examine what went wrong with the last one.

"And there's the Marion-Edward love," she said once, sitting across from me, her fingers against her mouth the way they always were when she was thinking. "When a person thinks they know somebody inside out and then boom—one day she just ups and leaves. Thing is *knowing* and *loving* are different."

"Do you think they ever loved each other, Anne?"

Her eyes grew dark then, serious. "Once. Maybe. A long time ago. They were so excited about it, they jumped right in. And then they were lost." She shrugged. "And now they're old—and each is all the other knows—so they just hold on."

"To what?"

She shrugged again. "To whatever."

Then we were silent for a while. I sat against the fireplace imagining my mother and father in the middle of the ocean, stuck out there, but each keeping the other above water.

"And sometimes," Anne said softly, "there's just plain love, Ellie. No reason for it, no need to explain."

Then she leaned back on the couch, crossed her ankle over her knee, and grinned. "Perfect love," she said.

"And what's that like?"

"When you find it, lil sis. You'll know."

Some mornings, there is only this in the world—Jeremiah's hand reaching for my own. There isn't Marion's warning about time making changes we can't ever anticipate. Only Miah's hand in mine and a voice much louder than Marion's—my own—saying, *Take this moment and run, Ellie.*

Take this moment and run.

Chapter

16

It snowed the morning he met Ellie at the library. Jeremiah climbed the stairs slowly, lifting his knapsack higher up on his shoulders as he walked. He had always loved this library with its two stone lions guarding the Fifth Avenue entrance. When he was little, his mama would bring him here and they'd sit for hours reading poetry in the quiet high-ceilinged rooms.

Ellie was leaning against one of the lions, the collar of her pea coat pulled up around her ears, her eyes soft and bright. She had braided her hair, one long neat braid that fell from beneath the ski cap she wore down across her back. Jeremiah made his way toward her, feeling clumsy suddenly.

"You look nice," she said, leaning forward to kiss him. He smiled then, relaxing. She made him feel all right. Everytime she smiled or kissed him or called his name in the hallway, he felt it. That everything everywhere was going to be all right.

"You too," he said.

They stared at each other without saying anything.

"It's snowing," Ellie said. "Can you believe it?"

He shook his head. Above them the sky was dark, blue-gray. Ellie's eyes changed with the weather. Now they too were blue-gray, like smoke.

"You want to go inside?" The snow was starting to come down harder.

"No."

"Me neither."

Around them, people rushed up and down Fifth Avenue.

"I guess we have to though, huh?"

Miah shrugged. "Yeah. Guess. Still doesn't mean I want to."

Ellie smiled, then leaned forward and kissed him again.

A black woman eyed them suspiciously as she

headed into the library. Jeremiah felt Ellie's hand close tighter around his own.

"You think it'll always be like this, Miah?" she asked after the woman had disappeared through the door. "The looks and people saying stuff. I hate it. I mean, I really hate it." She sighed, pressing her head back against the lion.

He nodded, loving this about her too—that in the little bit of time they'd been together, Ellie had come to see it, to understand how stupid the world could be sometimes.

"I think of it . . ." Jeremiah said slowly. "Like weather or something. You got your rain, your snow, your sunshine. Always changing but still constant, you know?"

Ellie frowned, shaking her head. "That's a bit too deep for me."

She shivered and Miah pulled her closer to him. "Let's say it's rain—the people who got problems with us being together—let's call them and their problems rain."

Ellie nodded. "Okay, they're rain." She smiled. "So now what?"

"So it's not always raining, is it? But when it's

not raining, we know the rain isn't gone forever."

Ellie sighed. "Well a drought would be a beautiful thing."

He wiped the snow melting across her forehead. "Let's go inside."

Ellie lifted her knapsack higher onto her shoulder and followed him.

"You can't own it," Jeremiah whispered, leading her to a nearly empty table. He shook out of his coat and draped it over the seat next to him. "If you just carry that stuff around with you all the time, it eats you up."

Ellie raised an eyebrow at him as she took off her hat and smoothed her hair back.

"It eats me up even if I don't own it," she whispered, placing her own coat on the chair beside Miah's and sitting down. "I just wish that part of it—would go away."

"It only goes away if we go away, Ellie. From each other."

She looked down at her hands. "You know something? That first time when we were sitting in Central Park talking—and then you cut that Snickers bar right in half and handed me that piece—I was thinking this is what I've waited forever for—you know—somebody I could talk to, somebody who *got it* the way you get me. And there you were, not even a foot away from me, listening and sharing your candy." She was thoughtful for a moment. "When I used to dream about that somebody, they never had a face. It was more like a feeling. I didn't know it would be like this—this good and this hard."

"What if you had known?"

Ellie looked away from him. "I would have still come—still tried to find you that day in the hallway. Isn't that crazy? Because that stuff, that junk—the looks and words—I would . . . if someone told me that's what I had to go through . . ." She smiled and put the end of her braid into her mouth. "To get to you. I would've still kept on coming."

"Me too," Miah whispered. "No question."

Chapter 17

"THING ABOUT WHITE PEOPLE," HIS FATHER WAS SAY-ing. They were driving along the Long Island Expressway, heading out to East Hampton. There was a house there his father wanted to look at for his next film. "They don't know they're white. They know what everybody else is, but they don't know *they're* white." He shook his head and checked his rearview mirror. "It's strange."

Jeremiah stared out the window. How had they gotten on the subject? He didn't want it to be like this when he told his father. He didn't know what he wanted. Maybe he wanted his dad to hug him and say, "I'm proud of you son, for doing what's in your heart." But he hadn't even gotten to the Ellie part. "Maybe some of them know it."

His father eyed him and smiled. "When they walk into a party and everyone's black, they know it. Or when they get caught in Harlem after nightfall, they know it. But otherwise . . . Okay, take this black church thing . . ."

Jeremiah nodded. He knew all about the recent bombings of black churches. A new church was bombed almost once a week now. Everybody in Fort Greene was talking about it.

"A white person reads the paper and says, 'That's too bad for those churches. It's a shame. I hope they catch that person soon.' "

Miah shrugged. "What else can a person say. That's what *I* say."

"That's true. But you also have to take it a step deeper 'cause you're black. They're not 'those churches,' they're *black churches* and because they're black churches, they affect you." He took one hand off the steering wheel and pointed to his heart. "In here. Deep."

Miah turned back to the window. Last Saturday, after they left the library, he and Ellie had been walking along Fifth Avenue holding hands when these white boys started acting stupid—saying stuff like "jungle fever" and "who turned out the lights?" Miah had clenched his jaw and held tighter to Ellie's hand. *Walk through the rain*, Ellie had said.

"You don't think there's one white person in this world, Daddy," Miah said now, "somewhere—who's different? Who gets up in the morning, looks in the mirror, and says, 'I'm white so what am I gonna do with this—how am I going to use it to change the world?' "

His father frowned and thought for a moment. Then his face softened. He reached over and took Miah's hand.

"You know what Miah-man," he said. "I truly, truly hope so."

Chapter 18

"CAN YOU EXPLAIN THIS TO ME, MISS ELISHA?"

I looked up from my science book. Marion was standing in the doorway holding a small white card.

"Explain what?" It was Saturday morning. Later, I would meet Miah downtown and we'd see a movie. But right now Marion was standing in the doorway, dangling a white card between her thumb and forefinger as though it were something dirty, something that shouldn't be touched.

"This *absence*." She held the card up and read:

"Dear Parent. Please be informed that your child was absent from her Trigonometry II class on Thursday, October 22."

I shrugged. October 22. The first time we kissed. Had it really been that long ago. That beautiful day in Central Park. How did time move so quickly without moving at all? "I didn't go. What's there to explain?"

"But you were at school that day."

"Yes." I laid my book on my lap and looked out the window beside my bed. I didn't want this—to have to explain. Not to Marion. Not to anybody. Who would understand? He was Miah. Jeremiah Roselind. And when we walked out of Central Park that afternoon, he had taken my hand in his and held it. Who would understand that in this stupid family—the way our hands looked together—dark and light all at once. The way his hair felt so different from my own. Who in this family of people who married people who looked just like them would ever *get it?*

"Elisha," Marion said. "I'm talking to you!"

"Of course I went to school that day. I just didn't go to trig."

"Elisha," Marion said, so softly it surprised me. "Don't do this. Please don't do this. Don't do it to me, don't do it to your father. We don't deserve it."

"What do you deserve, Marion? You went

away—just left—boom—out of here. Twice. I think I can miss a forty-five-minute class and not have to explain it."

"Are you always going to hold it against me?"

I glared at her.

"We always wondered when you'd get angry about it," she said. "Everyone else got angry, but you never did." She held up the card. "So I guess this is anger then."

"You don't know anything, Marion. My not going to trigonometry has nothing to do with you. Believe it or not, everything isn't about you."

She turned to leave, then stopped.

"I think I know a lot of things, Elisha. I know everything isn't about me. Maybe you think you have all the answers right now because of that boy, but you don't. You'll see how your life turns around on you and sets you down in some strange other place."

"I have to study. And there isn't any boy."

"The one that calls."

"That's just a friend from school."

"You'll see, Elisha—how life plays tricks on you," she said again.

I stared out the window for a long time after she

left. All the leaves had fallen off the trees in Central Park and the sky was overcast and gray. I could see people walking hunched over, bending against the cold. I shivered. Marion was wrong. No, maybe she wasn't wrong, but she was slow. My life had already turned around and set me down in a strange other place. I ran my hand across the navy blue comforter that covered my bed. A beautiful, wonderful, perfect, perfect place.

Chapter 19

"YOU KNOW I'M LEAVING FOR L.A. FIRST THING tomorrow."

Jeremiah nodded and poured some cereal into a bowl. "You told me last week. We got any orange juice?"

"Should be." His father was sitting at the table, the *New York Times Metro* section opened in front of his cup of coffee. He gave Miah a puzzled look. "You okay?"

"Yeah. Just tired."

"You were out pretty late last night. What time you get home?"

"Around ten." Miah poured some orange juice

over his cereal then brought the bowl to the table. He sat down across from his father.

"Speak to me Miah-man. What's happening in your life? Feel like I never get to see you. This the first time all week you stayed here and I thought this was *my* week."

"I had a lot of studying to do—and I knew you were having people over for dinner a couple of times. It's quieter across the street."

His father frowned. "Well, it'd be nice if you came in and met the people *then* went to Nelia's."

"I met those people last time. That big lady that kept flirting with me?"

"Who? Kate Mitchell?"

"I think that was her."

"Kate was in my last movie." He grinned. "She played the schoolteacher. She's just messing with you."

"I know." He looked around Lois Ann's kitchen. It was painted a pale green, with plants and pictures everywhere. He liked his mother's kitchen better— with its big windows and soft white walls.

"And where you going on weekends these days anyway?"

Jeremiah took another bite of cereal and chewed it slowly before answering. "Mostly go up to Central Park—hang out with some people from Percy." He hated lying to his father. Yes, he did go to Central Park, but it was to hang out with Ellie—to sit and talk with her for hours and hours.

"You be careful over there. No running."

Every since he was a little boy, his father had always warned him about running in white neighborhoods. Once, when he was about ten, he had torn away from his father and taken off down Madison Avenue. When his father caught up to him, he grabbed Miah's shoulder. *Don't you ever run in a white neighborhood,* he'd whispered fiercely, tears in his eyes. Then he had pulled Miah toward him and held him. *Ever.*

"Times are different, Daddy," Miah said now.

"Not that different."

He knew his father was right. Knew by the way people eyed him and Ellie when they walked holding hands. It scared him sometimes. Those white boys making fun of them had scared him. He wasn't a fighter, had never learned how really. He didn't want to fight.

"I'm not running anywhere, just hanging out. When you coming back?" He asked, wanting to change the subject.

His father frowned again. "You know how those people are. They run you ragged. I'm trying to get over to TriStar or someplace where I can make some real movies instead of these fool pictures they've got me making now about fake blacks. Couple other studios say they want to do the same thing but talk is talk. Figure I'll get out there and see what people have to say about this new script—it's about a family and all the stuff they have to go through. No shootings or drugs, just everyday family stuff. Probably won't get too far."

Jeremiah ate slowly. He didn't feel like listening to Hollywood talk this morning. When his father got nominated for an Oscar last time, he got a studio deal—one of the big Hollywood studios said they'd give him the money to do whatever he wanted. But it turned out that wasn't the case after all. Now he was forever visiting other studios, trying to get away from the one he was with. Sometimes Jeremiah wondered why his father got married and had him. Yeah, he knew he loved him. But he loved making movies more.

"We saw a good movie last night. It was about bugs."

"Bugs?"

Jeremiah nodded and smiled. "A whole silent movie about insects. It was cool."

"What was the social message?"

"I guess that you shouldn't take bugs for granted."

His father rolled his eyes.

"Well, you shouldn't. You look up one day and there won't be a single bug."

"Good," his father said. "No roaches."

"No roaches. No aphids. No ladybugs. No honey-making bees . . ."

"No sweater-eating moths."

"No butterflies, no dragonflies, no fireflies lighting up the night."

His father laughed. "That's where you'd be a sad one. Remember how you used to catch all those jars of them down south? Mama'd make you take them right back outside and set them all free."

Jeremiah smiled, remembering those hot summer evenings down south—so many fireflies flicking off and on—their tiny specks of green light floating past him. All he had to do was reach out his hand and he'd catch one. Once, he and his cousin Frank had killed a bunch and smeared the green all over their hands and faces until they glowed. Then they had laughed as they ran along the road, scaring little children. His cousin Frank was three years older than Miah but that summer, it had been hard to separate them. Now Frank was at Moorehouse, playing football and majoring in sociology. The last time he had seen him was at their grandmother's funeral. Sometimes he got a feeling deep, like there were certain people he'd never see again. He felt that way about Frank. He should call him, just to say hey.

"Sometimes I get to missing people," Miah said softly. "I miss Grandma all the time—even though she passed four years ago."

His father sighed and nodded. "Yeah, I miss her too. My mama was something else."

"I start wondering what she'd say about all this— about us living the way we do."

"She'd understand. Me and Nelia were outgrowing each other. That happens sometimes. And while we were in the middle of outgrowing each other, I fell for Lois Ann. It's not right, but it's what happened." His father was quiet for a moment. "I never made a plan to hurt Nelia the way I did. It just happened," he said.

Jeremiah shook his head and stared down at his empty cereal bowl. He would never outgrow Ellie. She was inside him, all around him. Just closing his eyes, he could feel her hair against his face. He couldn't imagine never kissing her again. He couldn't imagine never wanting to. Or making her cry. That would tear him up inside, to see Ellie crying and know it was because of him.

"Daddy?"

"Hmm . . . ?"

"What do you think happens to people when they die? You think they just go back to the dust or you think it's something bigger?"

"I don't know . . ." He frowned, thoughtful. "I like to think it's something bigger, better maybe. But sometimes I think people just need to believe that to feel good."

"Some days I feel Grandma though. It's like she's right here." He touched his shoulder. "And she's whispering to me, telling me that it's all right where she is now. It's good. That she's happy." He

147

grinned and looked at his father. "You think that's crazy?"

His father shook his head and smiled. "Nah, Miah-man," he said softly. "I don't think that's crazy. I don't think that's crazy at all."

Chapter
20

I HAD BEEN TO BROOKLYN ONCE. WHEN I WAS SEVEN, Marion took us to visit her great-aunt. The twins were still living at home then. All morning they had argued with my parents. Neither of them wanted to go. I sat at the kitchen table, eating a bowl of Cheerios, dressed and ready. They had been to Brooklyn before, had visited the aunt a couple of times before I was born.

"We've done that already," Anne had said. "I have no interest in spending a Saturday afternoon sitting around that cramped Flatbush apartment."

"Me neither," Ruben had said from behind the pages of his history textbook. "And I have a ton of homework anyway."

"You're going," Marion said. "Everybody who lives in this house is going."

"You really want to see where I live?" Jeremiah asked nervously. We were sitting in the bleachers waiting for basketball practice to begin. Other players drifted in noisily. There were a couple of other girls scattered around the gym. We all knew that the minute the coach walked in, we'd all be kicked out. I crossed one ankle over the other and stared down at my loafers.

"Of course I want to see it, silly. You make Fort Greene sound like the only place in the world."

Jeremiah grinned. "It *is* the only place in the world. The only place I'd live." He grabbed my ankle and held on to it. "It'd be cool if you came to Brooklyn."

"Then it's a plan. When do you want me to come?"

"Come now."

I raised an eyebrow at him. "Somebody has practice, Miah. And it's not me."

"After practice. I'm done at four-thirty. We can take the train there." He winked at me. "I'll have you at my house by dinnertime."

I could feel myself blushing. "You're such a gentleman."

"Anyone not on the team—out!"

I looked up to see Coach standing in the center of the gym. Slowly, people started filing out.

"I'll meet you out front," I said, kissing my finger and touching it to his face.

He grabbed my hand and kissed it. "Four-thirty—Ellie Eisen heads to Brooklyn."

That time I had gone to Brooklyn with my family, I hadn't thought much of it. My great-aunt's apartment was cramped and dark and smelled of unbaked bread and morning breath. I had sat between Ruben and Anne while my parents talked to my great-aunt in low whispers—about the weather, their various aches and pains, and long-dead family members. My great-aunt served us weak tea and graham crackers. Then Marion evil-eyed us until we each had a cracker and had mumbled thank-you's. Then she eyed us a minute longer until we each took a bite of cracker and a sip of tea. Content, she went back to discussing the state of age-old affairs with my great-aunt. That was a long time ago.

As Jeremiah and I walked through the gate, I

felt my stomach dip at the idea of returning to Brooklyn again—a different Brooklyn. Jeremiah's Brooklyn.

"Is it near Flatbush?"

Miah shook his head and smiled. "That's like asking is the Upper West Side near Soho. Yeah—they're in the same borough, but there's a little bit of space between them." He was still sweating from working out. His eyes were bright the way they always were after practice.

"You call your moms?"

I nodded. I had lied—well, half lied—and told Marion I was staying late to work on something with another student.

"You call yours?"

Miah nodded. "Right after I stepped off the court. She said she'd make us a burger—You eat meat?"

I nodded.

"Well, that's too bad because my moms is like me. It'll be one of those soy burgers. They're good though."

"Yeah, right," I said, making a face.

Miah laughed. "Well, you're still gonna have to eat every bite so you don't hurt Nelia's feelings." He leaned over the edge of the platform. "Train's a-coming. That's what my dad always says. You nervous?"

I nodded. The train was loud and crowded. Miah had to lean into me to speak. He smiled and touched my cheek. People stared, but we made believe we didn't notice. People always stared. *I feel like I've grown an extra leg since we started going out*, Miah said once.

"Don't be nervous. Nelia's cool."

"What about your dad's house. Are we going there?"

"He's away on business again." He got quiet.

"How come you don't talk about him so much, Miah? And how come he's always gone?"

He shrugged. "I'll tell you when we get off."

It was cold when we came up out of the subway. I shivered and Miah put his arm around me for a second then let it drop back at his side.

The streets were quiet and still as we walked. "So many trees," I said. I hadn't remembered Brooklyn having so many trees. "It's pretty here."

"Yeah." He looked distant and worried. "Ellie," he

said softly. "You ever saw that film *Somewhere on This Journey?*"

I nodded. I had gone to see it with Anne and Marion last year after it had won something big at some film festival. Marion had cried clear through it. "That was a really great film."

Miah looked at me and took a deep breath. "My father made it," he said slowly.

I stopped walking and grabbed his hand. "Your *dad* is Norman Roselind?"

Miah nodded, looking away from me.

I let go of his hand and starting walking again. I felt strange suddenly, hot and cramped. For some reason I didn't want Miah to be Norman Roselind's son. I wanted him to just be Miah—a boy from Brooklyn. But he *was* Miah. But he wasn't.

"Ellie," he said, catching up to me and touching my shoulder. "There's more." He kind of laughed, but it was a nervous laugh—sort of tearful and scared at the same time.

"Remember when you were talking about that book Ms. Lanford is assigning in English Comp. The one about the girl growing up in Chicago?"

I nodded.

"My mom wrote it. She's written a couple of books."

We stopped walking again. I pulled my bottom lip into my mouth and chewed on it a moment. "Jeez, Miah. I thought you were—I thought you were just Miah."

"I *am* Miah. That's why I don't talk about them so much. When my mother and father split up, it was all over. Everybody knew. I hated opening up some stupid magazine and seeing myself in it—the poor only child of Norman and Nelia Roselind. I'm not some poor only child, I'm *Miah*." He swallowed. For a minute I thought he'd start crying. I didn't want him to start crying. If he'd started crying—I'd start crying. Or maybe I wouldn't. Maybe I'd just get on the train and go home—home to Marion and my father and my quiet bedroom looking out over Central Park. Home to our apartment where no one was famous or brilliant.

"I don't want you to go home, Ellie," Miah said.

"Who said anything about going home? I didn't say anything about anything."

"I can see it on your face . . . that . . . that you want to go home."

155

I lifted my knapsack higher on my shoulder.

"You could have told me sooner, you know. I feel like you've been lying—"

"But I *haven't* been, Ellie. I just didn't want to talk about them."

"Lies by omission." I turned away from him then. People going into the train station eyed us, but I didn't care. I hated being lied to. Hated it.

Jeremiah sat down on the curb.

"What if I had told you the truth from the beginning?" he said. "You would have thought I was something—somebody, I wasn't. That day, in the hallway, I wanted you to see . . . to see *me*, Ellie. Miah." He sighed and started picking at the tar. I watched him a moment.

"You could have taken a chance, Miah," I said. "Given me the benefit of the doubt."

"But that's what I'm doing now."

I sat down beside him and sighed. "I know. I mean, I know but I don't know. I would have worn something different if I had—"

"But I don't want you different, Ellie. I want you as you. The Ellie from the hallway with her hair and books falling everywhere. The Ellie who smiled at me—a real smile not something painted on your face."

I looked at him, feeling myself start to smile a bit, and shook my head. "Is there anything else? Is your uncle like president or something?"

Miah smiled. "Nah—not yet anyway."

I stood up. "Then let's go get those soy burgers. I'm starting to freeze out here."

Chapter
21

"Yo, Miah! Wait up!"

Miah turned and shook his head. "Figures."

Carlton ran up to them, his knapsack bouncing over his shoulder. "Tech beat Stuyvesant, man—one-ten to ninety-two. We squished them!" He held up his palm and Miah slapped it then watched Carlton's eyes slide over to Ellie.

"How do you do? I'm Carlton," he said, bowing.

Ellie smiled. "Ellie."

"The pleasure is mine, Ellie."

"Okay, Carlton. It was nice seeing you, hint, hint." Miah took Ellie's hand and started walking.

"This is the nice young lady from that first day,

158

isn't it?" Carlton grinned. "The one whose books you knocked out of her arms. Did he apologize, Ellie?"

Ellie laughed and Miah knew she liked Carlton. It made him feel good to see her laughing like that, to know his homeboy made her laugh.

"He apologized a couple of times actually," Ellie said.

Carlton climbed the stairs of his brownstone slowly. "Good, that means I taught him right."

He gave Jeremiah a power sign and made his way into his building.

"Well, that was Carlton," Miah said. "And here's one of my houses. Daddy lives right there." He pointed across the street.

Ellie turned and shook her head. "That's so wild."

"I think he'll move to L.A. though eventually. Probably not until I'm in college or something. But I think he'd rather be there."

They climbed the stairs slowly, Jeremiah walking a bit ahead of Ellie. The house was quiet and smelled of garlic and bread. "Think my moms bagged the soy burgers."

Ellie smiled. "This place is beautiful," she whispered.

"It's not a museum," Miah whispered back. "We don't have to whisper. Ma!"

His mother was sitting in the living room, a stack of paper and a pen on her lap. Miah bent to kiss her then introduced them.

"Nice to meet you, Ellie," his mother said, rising. He had not told his mother Ellie was white, and now his mother raised an eyebrow as she held out her hand.

"Nice to meet you too," Ellie whispered.

"She got bit by the shy bug on the way in, Ma." Miah grinned, kissing his mother on the cheek. "I told her I'd give her a tour to relax her a bit."

Nelia took Ellie's hand and placed her other one over it. She held it a moment. Jeremiah smiled. He loved his mama—so, so much.

"It's good to have you here," she said.

"You working on something?" Miah pointed to the stack of paper beside her chair.

"I hope so. This book has been knocking on my head for a couple of weeks. I've been resisting, but now I'm seeing what it's got to say to me." She turned back to Ellie. "That's writer talk for 'Yes, I'm working on another book.' "

Ellie smiled again and stared down at her loafers.

"You didn't tell me your mother was beautiful," she whispered as they made their way upstairs.

At the top of the staircase, Miah kissed her on the lips and smiled. "Nobody says that about their mother. Not to other people."

"She likes me. It wasn't weird. I was afraid it was going to be wei—This place is amazing!"

From the top of the stairs, they could look down into the living room and on past it into the family area. His mother had a fire going in the fireplace, and from the top of the stairs, the smell of wood burning mixed with the other smells in the house. They went from room to room, slowly, Miah opening doors that hadn't been opened in months.

"I'm gonna kiss you in each room," he said. "Then it's dinnertime."

"How many rooms to this place?" Ellie asked, her eyes wide.

Miah shrugged. "I'm not counting."

Chapter 22

By December, it was too cold to hang in Central Park. Miah and I spent Saturday afternoons at Nelia's, sitting in front of the fireplace with our school books spread out around us. Miah was smarter than me and this made me work harder than ever. By the end of the first trimester, neither of us had received a grade lower than 97.

"Am I ever gonna meet your family?" Miah asked one Saturday afternoon. Outside it had started to snow. There were windows on either side of the fireplace and often I found myself staring out of them, wondering what it had been like to grow up in such a place. The winding stairs at the other end of the living room were marble and wood. Some afternoons I ran up and down them in my bare feet, loving the way the cool marble felt, feeling like a ten-year-old, while Miah watched me from his place on the floor.

Now, staring out the window, I thought about my own apartment, how small and cramped it felt compared to this place. Yes, it was big—more space than the three of us needed, but it wasn't this. It was pretty, not beautiful. And my parents in it were aging and set in their ways, not elegant and creative like Miah's. Doctor's daughter. All my life I had heard how lucky I was to be so. I had never imagined anything different, until now, until I met Miah.

"I used to think my family would accept anybody," I said slowly. "No matter what color they were. I'm not so sure of that now." I looked at him and swallowed. "It scares me. I mean, a part of me doesn't want to find out."

"If we're gonna be together, you gotta find out, you know."

I nodded and turned back to the window. I had not spoken to Anne again. Maybe I was afraid of that too—afraid to find out that she didn't like the *idea* of me and Miah together. And what was at the heart of it all—that was the scariest part.

"If they have it in them, to not like somebody because of their color—then I might have it in me."

Miah moved closer to me. Upstairs, I could hear music coming from Nelia's office. It was soft music, air mostly, with fragile notes on the edges of it.

"I get scared of that too," he said. "About myself. That it's there someplace, ready to spring out—'cause sometimes—like remember that time those two old ladies on Fifth Avenue?"

I nodded.

"Times like that, I hate white people. Then I have to ask myself, How can I hate white people and love you?" He smiled. "And I don't know how to answer that."

We didn't say anything for a long time. Outside, the snow was coming down harder. I knew I would have to leave soon. And didn't want to. On days like this, I was afraid to leave Miah. Afraid I'd never see him again. Would I always be like this? Would I always be this afraid?

"Maybe I'll be a filmmaker," I said. "Or an artist. I would love to sit and paint for hours and hours."

"I didn't know you painted."

I smiled and looked at him. "I don't. Once I took a class and I was terrible. But I took it because it was the only class with openings at the summer camp I went to one year, so I was kind of forced into it. I wanted to take tap, but it was full. But I never imagined it—that if I wanted to, I could be some kind of artist. Not until—not until I met you really."

I picked up his hand and kissed it.

"My sister's girlfriend is an artist but nobody in my blood family." I had told him about all of them, about Marc and Susan, Anne and Ruben. Even about Stacey and my twin nieces.

"I wouldn't be an artist," Miah said. "At least not a filmmaker or writer. People would say, 'Oh, he just got that film made because of his father,' or 'He just got that book published because of his mother.' Stuff like that."

"What do you want to be—and don't say a basketball player!"

He laughed. "That's what I *dream* of being—my secret dream. Go pro. Make the NBA. Get Most Valuable Player. Have some basketball shoes named after me. I'd walk down the street and hear little kids saying, 'My mama's gonna buy me some Jeremiah Roselinds.' I'd tell them they had to make them burgundy and gray—or whatever they call it—in memory of Percy Academy."

"Then after you wake up from the dream," I said. "What would you want to be?"

Miah looked down at his hand. He stretched it out, then made it into a fist, then opened it again. "I don't know," he said softly. "I look into the future and I don't see anything else. It's like it's this big blank space where I should be. Isn't that weird?"

"What—that you don't have any real plans for the future? No, it's not weird—it's pathetic."

"So when do I meet the family?" he asked again. "You know—we can do one of those guess who's coming to dinner numbers."

I shook my head. "It's not only about you being black, Miah," I said. "It's about—I don't know. You're *mine*."

Miah smiled.

"They'd go crazy if they knew how much time we spent together. They'd have you over there down on your knees proposing to me."

"I'd do that. Carlton be best man. We'd get one of

your trillions of family members to be a bridesmaid. It could happen."

I leaned against his shoulder and smiled.

"You know something, Miah?"

"What?"

"I'd marry you tomorrow. Isn't that crazy? How much . . . you know, how much I love you?"

He shook his head and hugged me. And we sat there quietly, watching the snow make its way to the ground.

Chapter
23

THAT AFTERNOON, WHEN HE TOOK ELLIE HOME, HE kissed her good-bye at the corner. He had brought his basketball along for the ride and Ellie held it a moment as they stood in the snow.

"Your *other* girlfriend," she said, bouncing it. It made a dull sound as it hit the thin layer of snow covering the sidewalk.

"Keeps me company on the long trip home," Miah said, grabbing it from her and dribbling it quickly between his legs.

She watched him a moment. Then quietly, she pulled off her gloves, handed them to him, and reached for the back of her neck.

"Here," she said. "Turn around."

Jeremiah smiled, feeling the Star of David and the warm chain against his throat. "I'm not Jewish though," he said, turning back toward her.

She took her gloves back, kissed him again and started heading backward down the block. "I'm going to tell them about you," Ellie said. "You're going to meet them. Get ready. I love you." She threw him another kiss, then turned, ducked her head, and disappeared into the blanket of wind and snow.

Jeremiah watched her. He could still feel her hand on his neck. It felt good and warm and right. "Ellie," he whispered, grinning. "My Ellie."

He was too excited to get on the train right away and decided to cut through the park. He felt like he could run a hundred miles—like he could run to Brooklyn and keep going. Soon he'd meet her parents and know this whole other part of her. Of Ellie. His Ellie. Beautiful, beautiful Ellie. Who loved him.

He bounced his basketball slowly for a while, then started running with it, feeling as though he could lift up, fly.

Jeremiah didn't know that they had been looking for a man. A tall, dark man. If he had known, he would have stopped when the shout came from behind him. But he was tangled up inside his thoughts. Deep inside himself. All around him, the park was white with snow and brilliant but quiet. Empty. And dribbling his basketball quickly along the snow-covered path, he realized how much he loved the quiet. How much he loved Ellie. Yes, he did love Ellie. He would always love Ellie. And now running along the park in the early evening, no one else mattered—not his father and Lois Ann, not his mother's sometimes sadness, not even the layup he had missed at practice on Friday. Just Ellie. Just Ellie.

Miah bounced his basketball in front of him, his feet moving quickly along the path, so quickly he felt the hard ground inside his sneakers, heard his feet pounding, heard his own breath coming fast. *Keep your body behind the ball*, Coach had said. *Keep your palm above it*. Like Rodman. Like Julius Erving back in the day. *You could be great, Jeremiah. You just have to concentrate. Keep your mind and your body in the game*. And now he was in the

game, dribbling fast through the park, the late afternoon sun almost gone now, the patches of snow
moving quickly past him. And nothing else but the
ball and the feel of his feet against ground. And in
the distance, way off in the distance, Ellie smiling
from the bleachers and the team waiting for him to
score. He had to score.

"Stop."

But he couldn't stop. He was too close. He was
going for that layup again. This time he'd make
it. Two points was all the team needed and he'd
make those two points and be a hero, and Ellie
would rush to the floor and throw her arms around
him. Not caring who was watching. Not caring
who saw.

Jeremiah grinned. And in another moment he felt
his breath catch deep in the back of his throat. He
felt a slow burn of something—something hot and
hard against his side. And then he was falling, grabbing for the ball but falling, falling and losing control.

And in the yellow-gold light of the fading afternoon, Jeremiah remembered Ellie smiling up at
him, and he remembered his father's grin and his

mother's laughter. Already he was missing them. Like that afternoon alone in his mother's room. Again, just like that day, Jeremiah felt a sudden, terrible sadness.

And then nothing at all.

Chapter 24

OUTSIDE IT IS WINTER NOW AND BEYOND THESE stained-glass windows, the snow falls and falls. Gently. Now the sidewalk is almost covered. Snow for Christmas. The weatherman promises a white winter. Drape down over us, snow. Cover everything. Like a blanket. Like someone's hand on my back. Cover my eyes, snow—like Miah always did.

Guess who?

Miah.

Nope. Guess again.

Ahm . . . Miah.

Yep. How'd you guess.

Nelia stands tall and beautiful, her face calm behind a thin black veil. And at the podium, Miah but older, much older, lighter, and with someone else's eyes. Where are Miah's eyes? And then, I look back at Nelia and see them, looking at me, light brown, almost green eyes calm inside a dark face, so smooth. Smooth like Miah's, her head tilting toward me as if to say, *You loved him too, Ellie. I know.*

All around us—the sad dark faces with traces of Miah in them. Who are they? Cousins? Uncles? Aunts? Nelia's face is a familiar one. And the man speaking—his face familiar but vague—not Miah's face but a face from a newspaper, a television screen. Unflawed. So sure of himself, so calm and poised but the hands—shaking hands, hands with Miah's fingers.

And in the back, Carlton sitting with a girl who looks like him, but taller, older. A pale woman beside them and on the other side, a tall black man.

Beside me, Marion squeezes my hand. And on the other side, my father, sitting straight, looking straight ahead. Once I asked Miah if he ever forgot he was black. *No. I never forget,* he said. *But sometimes it doesn't matter—like I just am.* Then he asked me if I ever forgot I was white.

174

Sometimes, I said.

And when you're forgetting, what color are you?

No color.

Then Miah looked away from me and said, *We're different that way.*

And now, sitting between my pale mother and father, I cannot forget I am white with so many brown and black and gold faces around us.

This part—this gathering was for family, those close to Miah. But Nelia called me—had found my number in Miah's notebook, with the hearts drawn all around it. "We would like you to come," she said, her voice choking back tears.

Outside, journalists and photographers wait, wait to catch them—us—Miah's family—catch us in our sadness. I swallow. *This is my life at fifteen*, I am thinking, staring down at my hands. *Please world, stop this. I am only fifteen.*

His father is telling a story about Miah as a small boy. But I can't listen. All around us there are pictures—Miah in his Percy uniform, Miah with Carlton, smiling, a basketball on the ground between them. Miah with his team from Brooklyn Tech, with his mother and father. Even a small one—Miah with me. The two of us side by side on Percy's stairs, looking uncomfortable in our uniforms. But I don't remember who took it. I can't remember that day.

Someone blows their nose, hard. Beside me, Marion dabs at her eyes. *There is no boy, Marion. Not now. Not anymore.*

Marion offers me a tissue, but I shake my head. Let the tears come however they come, Norman is saying. I wipe my hand across my eyes, but they keep coming.

Now Nelia is singing, soft and beautifully about a sparrow somewhere watching over Miah. And, for the quickest moment, I see it—that bird. Coming softly toward me.

Chapter 25

And if you come I will be silent
Nor speak harsh words to you.
I will not ask you why, now.
Or how, or what you do.

We shall sit here, softly
Beneath two different years
And the rich earth between us
Shall drink our tears.

Chapter
26

THIS IS HOW THE TIME MOVES. IT IS JUNE NOW. IN A week, I'll be eighteen. In the halls and out on the stairs at lunchtime, other kids are making plans for prom and graduation. Prom. Graduation. Then Swarthmore in the fall. Marion and my father had been right—Percy Academy did get me into a good college. When the letter came, Marion held it up proudly. "A thick envelope," she said. "You know what that means." Yes, I knew what it meant. All spring the envelopes had been coming—thin ones meant one-page rejections. Thick ones meant acceptances and more paperwork.

There is a plaque outside the gym at Percy. It

reads *In Memory of Jeremiah Roselind. Somewhere someone will always be calling your name.*

I think only once in your life do you find someone that you say, "Hey, this is the person I want to spend the rest of my time on this earth with." And if you miss it, or walk away from it, or even maybe, blink—it's gone.

In our yearbook, there is a picture of me and Miah—sitting in Central Park—Miah has his lips poked out and is about to kiss me on my cheek. And I'm looking straight into the camera laughing. Two and a half years have passed, and still, this is how I remember us. This is how I will always remember us. And I know when I look at that picture, when I think back to those few months with Miah, that I did not miss the moment.

Marc and Susan are coming for graduation. Ruben is already here. And tonight, we drive out to Kennedy Airport to meet Anne and Stacey's plane. Then I'll return with them to California for the summer. And maybe one day Anne and I will talk about that evening on the phone. The first and last time we talked about Miah. That evening—a long, long time ago. When we were friends. When we were close. And maybe, once we talk about it, we'll begin to understand who we were then. Maybe we'll move toward each other again. Maybe.

Later, I will go to Nelia's. She'll read pages of her latest book to me. In the quiet afternoon, we'll drink tea and eat cookies and leave the room when we need to cry.

This is how the time moves—an hour here, a day somewhere, and then it's night and then it's morning. A clock ticking on a shelf. A small child running to school, a father coming home.

Time moves over us and past us, and the feeling of lips pressed against lips fades into memory. A picture yellows at its edges. A phone rings in an empty room.

And somewhere, somewhere there is this moment—me, opening the door to my apartment, calling to Marion and my father. They are in the living room—Marion is reading a book, my father the *New York Times*. When I walk in, I kiss them each hello, then sit down on the floor, my back against the fireplace.

"I want to tell you both something," I say, my voice shaking. "Today, I wasn't studying with friends. I was in Brooklyn. I was with a boy. His name is Jeremiah. He wants to meet you. Tomorrow."

Time comes to us softly, slowly. It sits beside us for a while.

Then, long before we are ready, it moves on.

Many thanks to the friends and family who helped me get this story on the page including Kathryn Haber, Nancy Paulsen, Patti Sullivan, Toshi Reagon, Teresa Calabrese, Catherine Saalfield, Susie Hobart, Elisha Hobart, Reiko and Miyako, Linda Villarosa, and Charlotte Sheedy.

JACQUELINE WOODSON

Behind You

PUFFIN BOOKS
Published by the Penguin Group
Penguin Young Readers Group, 345 Hudson Street, New York, New York 10014, U.S.A.
Penguin Group (Canada), 90 Eglinton Avenue East, Suite 700, Toronto, Ontario, Canada M4P 2Y3
(a division of Pearson Penguin Canada Inc.)
Penguin Books Ltd, 80 Strand, London WC2R 0RL, England
Penguin Ireland, 25 St Stephen's Green, Dublin 2, Ireland (a division of Penguin Books Ltd)
Penguin Group (Australia), 250 Camberwell Road, Camberwell, Victoria 3124, Australia
(a division of Pearson Australia Group Pty Ltd)
Penguin Books India Pvt Ltd, 11 Community Centre, Panchsheel Park, New Delhi - 110 017, India
Penguin Group (NZ), 67 Apollo Drive, Rosedale, North Shore 0632, New Zealand
(a division of Pearson New Zealand Ltd)
Penguin Books (South Africa) (Pty) Ltd, 24 Sturdee Avenue,
Rosebank, Johannesburg 2196, South Africa

Registered Offices: Penguin Books Ltd, 80 Strand, London WC2R 0RL, England

First published in the United States of America by G. P. Putnam's Sons,
a division of Penguin Young Readers Group, 2004
Published by Speak, an imprint of Penguin Group (USA) Inc., 2006
Published by Puffin Books, a division of Penguin Young Readers Group, 2010
This omnibus edition published by Puffin Books, a division of Penguin Young Readers Group, 2011

1 3 5 7 9 10 8 6 4 2

Poem on page vii from *All of Us: The Collected Poems* by Raymond Carver, copyright © 1996
by Tess Gallagher. Introduction copyright © 1996 by Tess Gallagher. Editor's preface, commentary,
and notes copyright © 1996 by William L. Stull. Used by permission of Alfred A. Knopf,
a division of Random House, Inc.

THE LIBRARY OF CONGRESS HAS CATALOGED THE G. P. PUTNAM'S SONS EDITION AS FOLLOWS:
Woodson, Jacqueline.
Behind you / Jacqueline Woodson.
p. cm.
Summary: After fifteen-year-old Jeremiah is mistakenly shot by police,
the people who love him struggle to cope with their loss as they recall his life and death,
unaware that Miah is watching over them.
ISBN: 978-0-399-23988-5 (hc)
[1. Death—Fiction. 2 Grief—Fiction. 3. Interpersonal relations—Fiction.
4. African Americans—Fiction. 5. New York (N.Y)—Fiction.] I. Title.
PZ7.W84945Be 2004 [Fic]—dc22 2003023179

Puffin Books ISBN 978-0-14-241554-2
This omnibus edition ISBN 978-0-14-241918-2

Printed in the United States of America

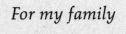

For my family

Behind You

And did you get what
you wanted from this life, even so?

I did.

And what did you want?

To call myself beloved, to feel myself
beloved on the earth.

—Raymond Carver

The Ending

Jeremiah

YOU DO NOT DIE. YOUR SOUL STEPS OUT OF YOUR BODY, shakes itself hard because it's been carrying the weight of your heavy skin for fifteen years. Then your soul lifts up and looks down on your body lying there—looks down on the blood running onto concrete, your eyes snapped open like the pages in some kid's forgotten picture book, your chest not moving. Your soul sees this and feels something beyond sadness—feels its whole self whispering further away. *Shhhh. Shhhh. Shhhh*—past the trees in Central Park, past the statues and runners and children playing on swings. *Shhhh. Shhhh. Shhhh.* Over yellow taxicabs and late-afternoon flickering streetlights. *Shhhh* away from the dusting of snow, the white tips of trees, the darkening sky. Already you hear your mother screaming. Already you see your father dropping his head into his hands.

Helpless. Already you see your friends—walking through the halls of Percy Academy. Stunned. But you do not die. Each breath your soul takes is cool and reminds you of a taste you loved a long time ago. Licorice. Peppermint. Rain. Then your soul is you all over again, only lighter and freer and able to be a thousand and one places at once. Your new soul eyes look around. See two cops standing there with their mouths hanging open. One cop curses and kicks a tree. Slowly your soul realizes it's in a park. There are trees all around you. And both cops look scared.

He's dead, one cop says.

And the other curses again. Your soul doesn't like the way the curse word sounds. Too hard. Too heavy in the new soul-light air.

The cops can't see you. They see a dead body on the ground—a young boy. A black boy. They know this is not the *man* they'd been looking for. They know they've made a mistake. Your soul looks at the boy and knows his friends called him Miah but his full name was Jeremiah Roselind. Tall. Dark. He has locks and the locks are spread over the ground. His eyes are opened wide. Greenish gray lifeless eyes. Your soul thinks—somebody loved that boy once. Thinks—once that boy was me. The wind blows the snow left, right and up. You are so light, you move with the wind and the snow. Let the weather take you. And it lifts you up—over a world of sadness and anger and fear. Over a world of first kisses and hands touching and someone you're falling in love with. She's there now. Right there. Look closely. Yeah. That's her. That's my Ellie.

The Hurting

Ellie

FOR A LONG TIME AFTER MIAH DIED, SO MANY PEOPLE DIDN'T
sleep. At night, we lay in bed with our eyes wide open and
watched the way night settled down over wherever we
were. I was in a room on the Upper West Side, in a house
my parents moved to a long time ago. Not a *house*—a
duplex *apartment* in a fancy building with a doorman.
My dad's a doctor. My mother stays at home. I go to Percy
Academy. Some people look at me and see a white girl in
a uniform—burgundy jacket and gray skirt—and think,
She has all the privilege in the world. I look back at them,
thinking, *If only you knew.*

If only they knew how we were sprinkled all over the
city—me in my big room, Nelia in her Fort Greene
brownstone, Norman in his girlfriend's apartment, aunts
and uncles and cousins, even strangers—all over New
York City—none of us slept. We lay there staring up at

our ceilings or out into the darkness. Or some days we stopped in the middle of doing something and forgot what it was we were doing. We thought, *Jeremiah's dead.* We whispered, *Jeremiah's dead.* As if the whispering and the thinking could help us to understand. We didn't eat enough. We peed only when the need to pee got so big, we thought we'd wet our pants. We pulled the covers off ourselves in the mornings then sat on the edge of our beds, not knowing what to do next. If those strangers looked, really looked into my privileged white girl face, they would have seen the place where I wasn't even there. Where a part of me died too.

Miah died on a Saturday afternoon. That evening, the calls started coming. First his mom, Nelia, asking if Miah was still with me. Then his dad, Norman. Then the cops. Then silence. Silence that lasted into the night and into the next dawn. Then the phone ringing one more time and Nelia saying, *Ellie, Miah's been shot. . . .*

I don't remember much more than that. There was a funeral. There were tears. There were days and days spent in my bed. A fever maybe.

There was no more Miah.

No more Miah.

No more Miah and me.

Nelia

I USED TO BE A WRITER. IDEAS AND PEOPLE AND PLACES WOULD come to me and I'd write it all down. There was such a *clarity* to the world then. When I sat down at my desk and began to write, I felt like I understood *everything*. I felt brilliant and whole and good. But who understands *everything*. Who understands *anything*. I mean *really*. People getting awards for being geniuses and brilliant writers and world shakers. Do they understand. Do they have any *idea* what it feels like to wake up some days not even sure of your own name. What is my name? . . . Nelia. It's Nelia. My whole name? Cornelia Elizabeth Roselind. But before it was Roselind, it was something else. This morning, I don't remember. It doesn't matter anyway. Who I was. Who I am. Who I'll be one day. You see, the whole world has changed for me. It's filled with people saying things I

11

don't understand. Faces on the television screen talk at me—lips moving with no sound. There's a war somewhere. And somewhere else, there are suicide bombers. People missing and found. Children looking for homes. Candy for sale. This morning, I saw a dog with only three legs. It was black and had the saddest eyes. But what dog isn't sad eyed. And what child doesn't want a home. My skin used to be so soft. But now I feel like a hard shell is growing over my blood and bones. *The New York Times* grows like a sunflower just inside the vestibule. It gets delivered in a blue plastic bag. A blue sunflower, growing out of control. But I can't stop it from growing. Someone needs to come to this house. Teach me how to dial a phone again. Because then I could call someone—who?—and say—what? Please don't deliver any more papers. Is that what you say? When a person answers the phone—do you ask for *less* of something? Who wants *less* of something? Don't we all want more?

I am not old. My hair is still black. The way it curls has not changed. Except in one spot. There. Right where the tiny indent of my neck bends into my head. The hair is straight there. Once it used to curl and the curls moved toward my neck. But now the hair sticks straight down like someone's bad perm job.

And my hands. I am not old, but my hands shake

sometimes. I cannot find a pen that writes. I cannot find paper to write on. I cannot. I cannot. I cannot.

So I sleep. In this big house with all of its quiet, what else is there to do?

Kennedy

Lost our last game up against Dalton last winter, 102–62. Dalton don't have no game. I mean, that team is *busted*. People trying to say it's 'cause Miah got kilt—killed—I mean, he got *killed*. But even if Miah's dead, that ain't no reason to get your booty *slammed* by some I-don't-want-no-scrubs from *Dalton*. I mean, show a dead brother some respect and at least go into some overtime or somethin'. Don't be just straight-up losing like that.

I'ma tell you—there's things I love about Percy Academy and stuff that be making me crazy. Like the team. I mean, I love ball, but Percy got the A-1 sorriest team this side of, I don't know—this side of the *galaxy*. Probably got a better team dribbling down the Milky Way. Three-inch Martians probably got better jump shots than the guys on my team. But there's stuff I love about that school too. Like—okay, so I know this is whacked and if someone said

I said it, I'd be ready to mess them up real bad and nobody'd believe them anyway 'cause everybody at Percy knows Kennedy don't be playing that, but . . . I love the uniforms. Carlos be saying, *There goes Kennedy in his monkey suit*, but I know it's just jealousy eating him up from the inside out. See, where I live, don't a whole lotta kids be going to private school. Kids be going to school— it ain't like how reporters be trying to televise—all that talk about high dropout rate and teenage pregnancy and blasé, blasé . . . Yeah, that goes on where I live, but it be going on where everybody else be living too. Only trouble is—the news got a need to be slanting stuff just to make people afraid. Like if peeps ain't running around scared enough as it is. I just hate that the news gotta be making people afraid of somebody that look like me. Or Miah. If Miah's really dead, then that's the reason—he's dead because of people being afraid. That's why I don't try to be afraid of nothing. In the morning I get up, brush my teeth, take a shower. I look in the mirror and take off my nylon, check my braids, make sure they working under- neath it. Maybe if my scalp's dry, I'll run a little bit of grease in the parts, spray a little oil sheen on my braids— you know, make them nice. Then I put on my Percy clothes: gray pants—I wear them baggy, the school don't trip, so that's cool—white shirt with a maroon tie. Maroon jacket got a Percy Academy patch on the left breast. Walk

15

out of building 1633 Albany Houses in NeverRan Never-Will Brownsville. Brooklyn, New York. Yeah—it's the projects. Yeah, I come from the projects. So what? Lots of Percy kids got heavy pockets, live in those big buildings on the Upper East Side and the Upper West Side. They be having doormen and dry cleaning dropped off and what-not. Stuff like that. I guess some of them probably think they better than me because they got some cash and what-ever, whatever. But truth is, cash and doormen and some nice clothes ain't gonna be going with you to the next place. Shoot—given the fact that we gotta wear uniforms at Percy, nice clothes don't even be getting you through *this* place. Yeah, I believe in a next place. And I believe in this place too. And when I'm sitting in my room, staring up at the posters of all the ballplayers that came before me—I start understanding that I know some things. I might not be real rich or real smart or real good looking, but I know some things. I know a cop shot Miah in the back and the bullet went straight through from his shoul-der blade to his heart. And then the heart just turned it-self off like a TV. And maybe it burned Miah to die that way. Maybe it hurt real bad going down like that. But some days, I feel my boy right here, right next to me. He's sitting on my bed. And he's looking up at the posters too. And he's got this big grin on his face. I even feel his hand—slapping mine, saying, *You know we shoulda whipped Dalton, yo.* And I take his hand, pull him to me real quick, slap his back. Say, *Who you tellin', Miah man? Who you tellin'?*

Norman Roselind

THE SNOW STARTED MELTING IN JANUARY. AFTER THAT CAME the rain. Jeremiah'd been dead about a month and a half by then. Each day, I looked out the window expecting to see some sun, but it didn't come for a long time. Shoot. It was like Miah died and the sun just changed its mind about shining. City so gray, it could've been Seattle. Pain in me so deep, some days I just stood wherever I was, my mouth hanging open, my eyes burning up. My heart always just banging and banging. All these years I hadn't thought about it, and then my son died and my heart started pounding, always, like it wanted to break right through my chest. Even as I'm telling this, it's banging. Doctors say nothing they can do about this feeling. And I know they're looking at me, wanting to say—*We can't bring him back, Mr. Roselind.*

So the world just stayed gray, my eyes burn, and then some days the tears come and don't stop, and then some days it's just my heart, banging and banging like that.

But I'm talking about that winter, right after everything. I was trying to do the things a person does to keep moving—dry cleaners, auto repair, post office . . . I'd taken a roll of film to get developed and when I got it back, there were some pictures in there from that day me and Miah had gone for a drive out to East Hampton because I was looking at this location to shoot my next movie. I don't want anybody to ever have to imagine what it's like to walk out of a drugstore with an envelope full of pictures under their arm—then, when they open that envelope, all they see is picture after picture of their dead son. I wouldn't wish that on anybody—no matter how deep my dislike of that person went. But that was me, walking up Fulton Street, my throat closing up so tight, I had to stop walking, remember how to breathe again. I remember a little girl and her mother crossed the street when they saw me standing there like that. Another woman asked if I was all right. I said, *My son . . . my son was killed. Jeremiah. My son was Jeremiah. He was only fifteen. Only fifteen.* I kept saying that. *Only fifteen.* And the tears came and wouldn't stop. The woman wanted to know what my address was and somehow I was able to tell her. She put her hand under my elbow and slowly led me home. Lois Ann was there. She thanked the woman. Took me upstairs and got me into bed. That was a long time ago. Some days it feels like it just happened.

In one of the pictures, Miah's got this big grin on his face. When I started going through those pictures, it took me right back to that day. Made me remember that we'd been having this whole talk about white people and I'd said something about white people not knowing they were white. Like if they go to a party, they don't know they're white if it's all white people in the room, but if they go to a party of black folks—*then* they know. I remember Miah getting quiet and staring out the window. He was wearing a green jacket and his black jeans. I remember looking over at him and thinking, *How did me and Nelia make such a beautiful child?* But he wasn't a child anymore. There was just the thinnest road of hair going across his top lip and his face had changed—he had my jawline—sharp. And he had the same habit I have of clenching his teeth when he was thinking real hard on something. We drove for a bit, him staring and clenching, me wondering what was on his mind.

"You don't think there's one white person in this world, Daddy," Miah said, "somewhere, who's different? Who gets up in the morning and says, 'I'm white, so what

20

am I gonna do with this—how am I going to use it to change the world?' "

Now I know why he was asking. Know why we were having that talk that day. But what good is it that I know now?

Jeremiah

THE SOUL LOOKS BACK AND WONDERS. MINE DID. ONLY I didn't know it was my soul—I thought it was me looking back at me. But I kept hearing my grandmother's voice. The way she'd say that—*The soul looks back and wonders*—every time something made no sense to her. Or every time I did something that seemed completely outrageous. Like the time I put a plastic snake on top of her laundry pile. She got so scared, she couldn't even catch her breath. And her sitting there with her hand on her chest breathing hard in and out made me realize—even at seven years old—that I'd done something there wasn't any turning back from. That the way she was gonna beat my butt once she finally *did* catch her breath was gonna be like no butt whipping I'd ever felt before. Or would ever feel again, thank goodness. And later on, as she took the strap to my bare legs and sore behind, she kept saying,

22

"The soul"—*slap*—"looks"—*slap*—"back"—*slap*—"and"—*slap*—"wonders"—*slap*.

My grandmother could beat a behind, yo. That's no joke. She'd get this look on her face when you got fresh, or got caught playing with matches, or put a snake on her laundry. And the look was like "Where in God's name did you ever get an idea that that was the right thing to . . . " And then you knew. You knew it was all over for your behind. My mom and pops never laid a hand on me, but my grandma made up for their non-whipping parenting by letting me know every now and then that

"In order to be raised right, Jeremiah—you can*not* spare the rod."

I was her only grandchild and she loved me with this love so fierce, my pops used to say you could feel it coming on for miles. Soon as we got a call saying she was on her way up to New York, my pops would say,

"Stand still, Miah. You feel the love coming?"

Desire Viola Roselind

FOR EIGHT YEARS I WAS MIAH'S GRAM. BEFORE THAT TOO, I reckon. Feels like I've known him since before he got to the world—longer than he knew himself, truthfully. Seems like we'd been friends really—not gram and first-born grandson—somewhere before life on earth . . .

Life. On. Earth.

Think on that. Earth looks small from far'ways. I remember when I was a child and my daddy showed me a blue marble, those kind that don't just have blue in them but lots of other colors besides. He says to me, *Girl, look hard at this here marble, 'cause what you looking at is the whole wide world.*

And I looked hard at the marble and then I looked real hard at my pa and I reckon I must have been thinking that here's a man I always loved who's lost his mind.

We lived in Aiken then. A little brick house. You went

up three stone stairs and then you were on our porch. And there was a swing on the porch—old iron swing that squealed to high heaven every time you sat down on it and commenced to swinging. Well, you went up those three stone stairs and passed that porch swing and then you were at our front screen door. Then you were in our front room—hardwood floors, a big potbellied stove— stove warmed the house like you wouldn't believe. One year, my baby sister set fire to her own dress sleeve standing too close to the open stove door. The skin on her arm was never the same after that, and she carried that arm sort of different from the other. When she got to be a young woman, she never wore short sleeves—not even in the hottest months—because she was ashamed. Don't know if the shame come from the scars or from her childhood foolishness of sticking her arm in the fire. Reckon it had to be some of both. Guess that's my first recollection of how people hide their scars.

Girl, my daddy said, *I know you think I lost my mind, but this marble is how the world looks to everybody but us humans.*

I looked at the marble. I looked at my daddy. I looked around at our little brick house. Back and forth and back and forth like that till I must have looked some kind of foolish myself.

Sir, I said, *I reckon I don't know what you mean when*

you say everybody but us humans. Ain't nobody else but God to see.

Uh-uh, Sweet Pea, my daddy said. He'd been squatting down, sitting back on his haunches like a lot of people used to do. He'd sit that way, squatted down, 'cause he was tall—over six feet—and me and my sisters and brothers had gotten our mama's gift for not growing tall. I was the smallest in the family—tiny hands, tiny feet and body.

Well, my daddy stood up and looked down on me and let himself smile. He had a nice, big, white-toothed smile, my daddy did.

Close your eyes, my daddy said.

I did.

And just let yourself think, Sweet Pea. Think about this world without its color and sound and smells. Let your breathing stop a moment.

I did.

Now commence to breathing again and open up those eyes.

I did.

And here is the whole wide world again. But better now, isn't it?

I looked around, and I liked the way it felt to have everything back in its place, the way the room came back in view and the floor felt hard again. And my daddy

26

standing there grinning like he would be that way . . . always. . . .

And now, here I am—way on the other side of that story and that beautiful day. I grew up and I grew old and then I got sickly and I died. But before all that happened, I had me a son, and that son had himself a son. And he named that boy-child Jeremiah.

And some mornings, Jeremiah comes to where I'm sitting, rocking in this big maple chair, the cushion softer than any cushion should ever be, the wood smelling like it was cut only an hour ago, the air cool and gentle as a child's hand. And Miah sits down beside me and we look out before us where the rest of the world is hustling past—people doing what they need to be doing to get through their days.

And Jeremiah says, *Tell me that story again, Grandma, the one about the marble.*

And the love in my heart for that boy-child just fills up inside me and spills all over.

Ellie

THE FIRST TIME I TRIED TO WALK TO THE PLACE WHERE THE cops shot Miah, it was dark. Central Park is not a safe place at night. People have been mugged. Raped. One man was attacked by a group of kids who just wanted to see if they could get away with it—rich kids from the Upper East Side. Some of them got away, but three were caught. *We were just playing,* they said. *We didn't think it would end that way.* Well, that man didn't make it. I don't know what happened to the kids—kids my age—fifteen, sixteen. The news was all over the story for a while and then it wasn't anymore. Something else must've happened and the media's absolute glee followed that new thing. The park at night is dark and quiet, though. If it wasn't for the danger, it would be a beautiful place. I wanted to see where Miah fell. I wanted to listen—hear him crying out. Two months had passed since his dying. It was late February

28

and so cold, my hands hurt. I knew the place—the papers had reported the story for almost a month. There had been demonstrations—yet another black guy shot in a case of mistaken identity. But this had been different. According to the papers, Miah was not just some black guy. He was a rich kid. He was the kid of famous parents. He was loved and attended one of the most prestigious schools in New York City. I read every word, even when Marion tried to take the papers from me.

"You don't need to do this to yourself, Elisha," she said.

"Yes, I do," I said back. Yes, she is my mother. But she doesn't understand. How could she ever understand any of it? How could anyone know what it was like? It was all so damned useless. And the stupid papers—how dare they? How dare they measure one life against another.

The first time I tried to walk to the place where the cops shot Miah, a dog ran out from nowhere, then darted back into the darkness. I stopped, a long way away from that place—in the dark and in the cold. I stopped, hugged myself hard in the darkness.

And screamed and screamed and screamed.

Carlton

THAT SATURDAY AFTERNOON—I'LL ALWAYS CALL IT THAT. That Saturday. Not "The Day Miah Died." Not "The Day a Whole Lot of Us Changed Forever." Not "Saturday, December Eighth." That Saturday, the snow started coming down hard. I had been sitting on the stoop just thinking on things. That fall, I'd begun to realize this thing about me, this stupid secret thing that I knew I'd never live out or talk about. And then the fall was over and it was starting to snow. A new season. Different weather and the secret getting older and deeper. When the snow started falling, it was wetter and colder than I'd ever remembered it being. I had on a sweater and some jeans and my hiking boots. Maybe I had on a T-shirt underneath, but it wasn't enough. Even my fingernails were cold. I looked over at Jeremiah's building—every window except Nelia's study was dark. I knew Miah wasn't home, so I couldn't go over there. But I didn't want to go inside my own house. My mother was inside and she was probably reading on the couch. A romance novel. She was probably reading about a woman who fell in love with a man and lived happily ever after. The books with the shiny gold letters on them. Always white women. My mother's white and I wonder if she sees some part of herself in those books—wonder if she makes wishes. Or just lets herself get caught up in them before coming back to planet Earth to make dinner for me and my dad and start ironing her clothes for the next week of working. She teaches. My father plays music. They've been together forever. My sister's in England. Oxford. She wanted to get out of New York. Wanted to get away from our tiny family, I guess. Maybe I was thinking about all of this as I sat there shivering and singing real low. Maybe it's because my dad's a musician that I like to sing. There's always been music in my house. That day, I was singing "Landslide"—not the remake, but the old Fleetwood Mac version where Stevie Nicks really rocks it. Jeremiah always thought it was strange that I was such a Stevie Nicks fan, but her voice— her *voice*—it did something to you. And no one can do "Landslide" the way she does. My father had turned me on to that song. He plays piano and guitar and a couple of other instruments. He'd sit down with his guitar and just start strumming and singing that song. *Can I sail through the changing ocean tide? Can I handle the seasons of my life?* And there was always such a sadness in his voice, but nothing compared to Stevie's. When she starts going on about the landslide bringing her down, it snaps the heart. So I sat there, singing, trying to do what she did with that song.

But then something strange happened. I forgot the words. I had been hearing and singing that song my whole life, and there I was, sitting in the heavy, wet snow, not knowing the lyrics to a song that was like the *alphabet* to me. And I looked around, starting to feel a panic build up. The block was empty and getting dark. The snow was coming down hard. And then I remember thinking, *And where the hell is Miah?*

The Healing

Norman Roselind

SUNDAY MORNING, I HEAR THE SOUND OF THE *TIMES* HITTING the stoop. It's still early and looks like it's going to rain. My girlfriend's still asleep. I look over at her as I'm rising out of bed. Her hair's getting gray and her cheeks are starting to puff a little bit with age. Wonder what she sees when she looks at me. I look at my hands, the way they still shake most days, the way my whole body trembles sometimes until I think relaxing thoughts—oceans and forests and cool, lazy evenings. Still, my heart bangs against my chest. And my eyes, I know when a person looks into them, they see only half a man—not completely focused, not completely there. I touch my girlfriend's back, watch my trembling hand move down over it. She's a beautiful woman—brown skinned, dark eyed, enough meat on her bones not to ever be called skinny. Has a voice like something cool calling your name. The trembling slows, then stops, and I rise, pull my robe on over my pajamas and go downstairs to get the paper.

When I open the door, I look up at Nelia's window. I used to be married to her. And we used to have a son. I feel my hands start to tremble again and think, *That's the past now. Move on.* There's a dull ache in my head. I pull the plastic off the paper and look at the headlines without reading them. So much news. So many things to do in a day. So many people to remember. And birthdays and holidays coming up. Eggs and milk to buy. Miah wore a size eleven shoe. My hands. My head. Lake Erie. Lake Champlain. The way the water laps against the shore on Montauk. Miah's brown hands building a sand castle. His thin seven-year-old body. *Daddy, look!* And the wave coming up that afternoon. The way he laughed as the castle melted into the ocean. Where was that? St. Croix? Mauritius?

Nelia's curtains are pulled—they've been that way for some time now. The papers were piling up on her stoop, but now they're all gone. She lives just across the street and a few houses up. It wasn't supposed to end like this. I wasn't supposed to fall in love with Lois Ann. Some things just happen and you feel them happening but you don't have a whole lot of power over them happening. You have to kind of give yourself over to them. Maybe me and Nelia were moving apart for a long time. It's hard to look back on. The edges of the past get fuzzy when I try. Moments come clear—the first time I heard my newborn son cry. The way his eyes changed to the same color as Nelia's and him with parts of Nelia and parts of me all running together to make some strange and wonderful whole new being. He really was *something*.

I sit down on the stoop and try to read the *Times*. The president wants a war. Some businessmen have been stealing people's retirement funds. A baby found, left beside a grade school. The baby's fine. The schoolkids all want her to be named after them. I read this story and even with all of its ugliness, I can't help smiling. Kids are something. All they can see is the beauty in a moment. I sit there like that awhile—every once in a while looking up at Nelia's window. Feel like I've been making films all my life and none of them can tell the whole story. I'd love to make one— just one—movie that goes from the beginning to the end—tell-all. And not that greasy talk-show tell-all kind of thing, but you know, go to the heart—to the heart's heart—and let the world feel everything deep like that.

Now the curtain in Nelia's living room moves a bit. I want to say, *Open the window, Nelia. Open the doors. Come outside. It's autumn.* This morning is cool and beautiful. The trees are starting to change color. *Look, honey,* I want to say. *Look how the world is moving on.*

Nelia

IT RAINED THE FIRST MORNING ELLIE RANG MY BELL. IN THE city, the rain makes the world gray and then the sun shines down on that gray and everything echoes of silver. Such a beautiful metal, silver is. And downstairs, Ellie stood draped in it, her thick black hair damp, her clothes wet, her long, thin body shivering.

It's Ellie, she said, looking up at the window. Looking up at me.

Then Ellie smiled. Her beautiful Ellie smile and a moment, a moment from a long time ago draped itself over me: my Jeremiah and Ellie in that spot where Ellie was standing. Ellie turning toward Jeremiah and offering my son that smile. I felt old watching them through the window. Old but excited—like I was fifteen again too and turning toward some boy—who would it have been?—and smiling.

"Ellie," I said. "Ellie, it's good to see you." My voice sounded so foreign to me. An old lady's voice. When had I become old? A birthday had passed, but still . . .

How long had it been since Jeremiah's last day with us—a month, two months, a year. Maybe Ellie knew. Maybe Ellie would tell me.

But once inside, she put her hands in the pockets of her jeans and looked around. The smile gone now. What was she seeing? The gray, dusty inside of what was once a beautiful home. The darkness. One by one, the lightbulbs had burned out. Now I flicked switches and got nothing.

"It's kinda dark in here," Ellie said. And then the smile was back. There was something different to it, though— embarrassment around the mouth and at the edges of the eyes. "How about we light some candles."

She followed me into the kitchen, where I pulled dusty white votive candles from a drawer.

"The matches are over the stove."

Ellie walked over to the stove. To the left of her was the window that looked out over our block. Yellow stained-glass panes across the top of it. A yellow linen curtain hanging from it. Dusty. Still. Ellie pulled it back, the matches in her other hand forgotten.

"He loved the light in this room," she said, her voice almost a whisper. I watched her thin hand reach up to the yellow panes, her pale skin soften in their light. In the cloudy rain-light coming in from the window, I could see that her fingers were long and the nails were painted a soft pink. I wondered when she had done this. Late at night? In the morning? Was she thinking of Jeremiah as she brushed the color on? Whom did she make herself beautiful for these days?

She kept her hand on the glass, oblivious of me. The kitchen grew terribly silent, a silence I had come to know too well. And now, with Ellie in it with me, the silence didn't seem to belong. But I stood there in it. Watching Ellie's hand touch the glass. I stood there, wearing the same khaki pants I had been wearing for I don't know how many days, the same white T-shirt I don't remember ever pulling over my head. The day after Miah's funeral, I marched to the Fulton Street Barbershop and had them cut off all of my hair. Who needed hair? Who needed anything? But now, I let my hand reach up to my head and felt that the hair had grown in some, long enough now for me to grab a handful of it. As I did this, something strange happened—the sun, which had been watery and elusive all morning, turned sharp and bright, spreading a thin layer of brilliant yellow over everything. I kept my hand in my hair and slowly looked around the kitchen—at the yellow dust covering everything, the cedar chairs draped in yellow light, the battered, beautiful wooden table with yellow swimming across it, the white walls looking as though they'd been dipped in butter . . .

Ellie turned then, and for a moment we just stared at each other. The air had left me. I felt ragged suddenly—hollow. I wanted to scream into the yellow light. Yet—it held me . . . up and together.

"He . . . ," Ellie said again, looking directly at me. "He really did love this light."

Carlton

SEPTEMBER. THE LEAVES ARE STARTING TO COME DOWN. THE sky—the sky seems like it's just *this* much closer to the earth. It's cool today but still warm enough for me not to wear a jacket. This—this is the kind of day a guy can fall in love with. If I could marry a day, it would be a day in September—the kind of day that makes you feel kind of blue and kind of crazy all at once. But you can't marry a day. My mother married a night. My father. Carlton Sr. Black man. And me, born a color somewhere between my blue-eyed white mother and dark-skinned dad. What if the color white was a day? And what if my mother had married a day instead of a night? Then I'd be all white. I wouldn't be walking through this September day, choking up at falling leaves. Would I be alone?

Someone dies and you hold on to everything you can. I think it's easier if you know they're gonna die—somebody old who you loved—like a grandmother or a sweet old uncle. You watch them die, you expect their death, and while death is coming, you're getting stories from them and touching their skin one last time and smiling and telling them how much you love them. But when someone gets killed—the way my homeboy Miah got killed—shot down by cops in a case of mistaken identity—sounds clichéd even to say it. Wish it was a cliché. Wish it was a dream that I could wake up from, shake out of my head and say, *Now where did that come from.* No. No dream. When someone gets killed, when that someone is this guy you've spent just about every day with since you were this high—well, then you don't see it coming. And all you have to hold on to is what you remember— and the day. The light of it. The weather. You in it. The way everything about it smells and feels and looks. Then you go to bed at night feeling like you lived it, really lived it. Like you walked through the world that day—whole. When somebody dies real quick and unexpectedly like Miah did, you spend every single day, after the news hits you, trying to live. And maybe sometimes you're living with some big secrets over your head or some big regrets in your heart. But the good part is you're walking and breathing and waving hello. And as the days go by and turn into weeks and months and years, you realize how much each day you get through matters.

I take a deep breath and keep walking. Still day. Windless day. Day with so much color to it, my head starts to ache. But then the color softens. It feels as though the whole sky is trying to wrap itself around me. I stop, lean against a mailbox and take small breaths. And it feels like the air is trying to breathe with me. *Calm Carlton*, the air feels like it's saying. *Why you gotta be so high-strung anyway.* But it's not the air—it's Miah. I hear his voice, feel him grinning. Then I'm grinning too. Headache gone quickly as it came. *Why you gotta be so high-strung.*

"Miss you, man," I whisper.

A little boy passing by me stops.

"You talking to me?"

He's brown like Miah. Clean-cut. Neater than any little boy should be.

I shake my head and he shrugs and keeps on moving. *You ain't all gone, are you, Miah?*

And the wind starts blowing, soft and high as a song.

At the corner of South Oxford and Fulton, a car swerves to miss hitting a small dog. I hear the dog's owner scream and watch her curse the driver out. Then he's cursing back and the cars behind him are honking and the day doesn't seem as beautiful as it did a minute ago.

I keep walking. When I get to Vanderbilt and Fulton, I stop and think about grabbing a cup of coffee. At a red light, some scrub leans out of the passenger side of a beatdown Honda and says *Hey, Girl-boy*. He winks at me. I hear the other guys in the car laugh.

"You weren't calling me that last night," I say. And wink back at him. The guys in the back start howling and the scrub gets so mad, he makes a move to get out of the car, but the light changes and his friend speeds off.

I keep walking. Girl-boy. Fag. Batty-boy. The list goes on. I've heard it all before. I remember me and Miah were walking this one time and some guy he knew from some-where pulled him to the side and whispered, loud enough for me to hear, "What you hanging with the sissies for, Miah-man?"

Miah had his ball in his hand—the way he usually did. He chucked it to me and grinned.

"Take some inventory, man," Miah said to the guy. "Everything in the world's just a little bit deeper than you seeing it."

The guy walked off without saying anything else. I know he didn't have a clue to what Miah was talking about, but maybe he walked on thinking about it some. I don't know.

Did me and Miah ever talk about this? About *it*. About who I really am—you know, way down deep beneath the me that's part white, part black, a ballplayer, a singer, a pretty-boy?

Nah. We didn't. We left that stuff alone. We talked

about ball and our folks and more ball. And when Miah started falling in love with Ellie, we talked about that— about what it meant to be a black guy who was loving a white girl. And once we got on that subject, it was like— well, it was like that's all there was, because he and I could spend hours just talking about people's reactions and his own fears and what it felt like to just be with Ellie. He loved that girl. I'd sit talking with him and then I'd come home to my parents sitting on the couch, watching TV— sometimes my dad would have his arm around my mom's shoulders. And I'd think, *Man, I can't even hardly imagine it, but these two old people were, like, our age one time and they got some of those same funky stares and comments Miah and Ellie got.*

So with all that going on, where was there a place to say, *You know, Miah, I don't think I'm the kind of guy that likes girls.*

But now that Miah's gone, I find myself having all kinds of conversations with him. Telling him when I first started feeling this way, how lonely I've been all these years, how all the stuff I don't say and don't do goes into ballplaying and that's probably why I'm on the starting five and one of the best ballplayers in the history of Brooklyn Technical High School. Stupid name for a school that's supposed to be one of the best in all of New York

City. Decent ball team, though, and some smart kids running through it.

I miss Miah so much, it hurts—real deep some days and other days it's just a hollowness. *You'll get close to someone again like that,* my mom said. It was one of those rare moments when we sat down at the table together—her drinking coffee, me eating a piece of leftover pie. But even though I sat at the kitchen table and nodded as she talked, on and on, trying to make me feel less of the sadness, I knew she was wrong—would always be wrong about that.

You won't always be the beautiful lonely boy you are, Carlton.

Beautiful-lonely—that's what my mother calls me. She knows even though we never spoke about it. She watches me watching people. Watches me walk and sing and talk. Comes to my games and watches me watching other ballplayers. She knows. Looks at me sideways and smiles a little bit when my father says, "When you gonna bring a girl up in this house for us to look at?"

"That's Carlton's business, isn't it?" my mother says. Because she knows. And she doesn't want my father to know before I'm ready to tell. Before I'm a hundred percent sure myself. About this. About that. About everything.

I wish I could love a girl the way Miah loved Ellie, but I just don't think about them that way—girls. I just don't. I try to force myself to—try to imagine my lips on a girl's, my arms around her waist, my hands making designs on her back. But the thoughts drip down into nothing. I feel . . . nothing. I am . . . nothing.

Jeremiah

IN A CLASSROOM IN A SCHOOL AROUND THE CORNER FROM where I grew up, a teacher is explaining death to seven-year-olds. Over the summer, the class hamster has died. A girl in the class has lost a beloved grandmother and another, an uncle. One kid remembers me and tells the class again how this guy he knows was shot by cops.

And he wasn't even doing nothing, the kid says. *Just running home from his girlfriend's house.*

Death, the teacher says. *Death is like sleep.*

Maybe there are twenty-five kids in the classroom—they're all colors because this neighborhood is changing fast. Even in the few months since I've died, it's changed. More white people moving in. Old black folks who've been here forever moving back down south or back to the Caribbean. The walls in this classroom are the same, though—painted pale blue. A poster on the wall—a kitten hanging from a bar—and underneath the kitten, the words HANG IN THERE. Another poster with the alphabet written in cursive. I remember being a kid and walking into this room, looking around wide-eyed, holding tight to my mama's hand. The room still smells like chalk. The chairs have names scratched into them. The desks are new, though, particle board and some kind of wood veneer that adds a new smell to the classroom, an unfamiliar one.

A little boy raises his hand. He could be me. Same dark skin. Same close haircut, shaped up on the sides and across his forehead. He's wearing a very white T-shirt and new-looking blue pants. His face is scrubbed and shining with oil. Today's the first day of school. Second grade. Twenty-something second-graders and all of them clean and excited and hungry for whatever is coming.

If death is like sleeping, the little boy says—his name is William, William Carlos—named, yes, for the poet. *If death is like sleeping, then how come dead people don't just wake up?*

I stare into his teacher's eyes. A flicker across them—she is stumped—but she recovers quickly.

It's a deeper sleep, she says.

Twenty-something pairs of eyes look back at her. Twenty-something children who won't sleep well tonight.

William Carlos looks at her. The others look at her, their mouths slightly open.

50

And then death comes, I want to say to them, *and you hang on.* And for a long time you don't even know you're dead and you're walking around in some strange place, staggering, asking everybody you meet—*Where am I? Where am I?* Then you see your long-dead grandma . . . and you know.

I want to let go—want to be whole on the other side of living. But life has a river running through it and we're all of us—dead and otherwise—on it together, linked up to one another. I want to stop looking. But I can't. I just can't. So I get up off that poor teacher's desk. Leave her sitting there with all those eyes on her.

When I was a kid, I learned this poem by Robert Frost and one of the lines in it was something about miles to go before I sleep. . . . Everybody seemed to have some different interpretation for that line. I don't remember the whole poem anymore, but I understand that line. If death is like sleeping, then I got a long way to go before I'm completely gone.

And that's what I'm thinking as I move out into the world. I turn and take one more look at William Carlos—his clear brown skin, his wide dark eyes. Future like a big empty trick-or-treat bag at the beginning of Halloween night.

Kennedy

IT TAKES ME AN HOUR AND FIFTEEN MINUTES TO GET HERE from Brownsville. Three trains, then a bit of a hike. But I've never been absent and I've never been late. My moms says, *Each day you go to that school is a gift, Kennedy*. She's never been up here. Says she don't have the right clothes. I didn't ask God to make me smart and a good ballplayer. He just did. And then lots of schools was saying, "Come here." "No, come here!" And then I was at Percy. But my heart's in Brownsville—with my moms and my boys and the Albany Houses. No matter where I go, I'm always gonna come back there. Ain't gonna be one of those kids that be leaving where they came from behind and making believe they came from a better place. I know people look at where I live and think all kinds of negative about it. They see people with a lot of kids and guys playing their music loud and smoking spliffs and that kind of stuff. They see us with our hair braided and our pants hanging low and they just think we all bad and whatever. My pops used to get mad when people would say I was "gifted." He'd say, "Nah—me and his mama the ones who got the gift—God sent us Kennedy." He used to think that was the funniest thing for some reason. And now some days I think about him saying that and I start grinning. The way my pops saw it, I was just like everybody else in these buildings—only thing is I got a real good game and somebody told me I was smart a long time ago and I believed it and started acting like it on paper—you know—doing my homework and stuff like that. Pulled down good grades. Teachers be surprised to see me with my hair braided, talking junk with my boys, then getting perfect marks on my spelling tests. My pops worked at a dry cleaner—pressing shirts and stuff. He didn't finish high school and he always wanted to go back or at least get a GED or something. It never happened, though. He used to say, "If somebody would go to each of the peeps up in these houses and say, 'You're something real special,' or something like that, no telling how many brothers and sisters would be jumping out of these doorways into college and probably even graduate school." I was a little kid then and didn't really believe him. But I do now. I don't know about being special or gifted or whatnot. I know *I'm lucky*, that's for sure. Ain't nothing special about luck—especially if you someone who doesn't have any.

Tuesday morning, I sat on the Percy stairs counting faces—white, white, white, white, white, Asian, Asian, white, black—Yo, what's up! (slap hands)—white, white, white, mixed kid—smiled at me, he's cool—white, white. . . . It went like that. When I got tired of counting faces, I took out some math homework and started looking it over, trying to wipe out the thoughts eating up my head. It was cool out—almost the end of September—one of those kinda days where you see a lot of people on blades and bicycles and walking around holding hands. The stairs go across the whole front of the school and even though the headmaster's always sending us notes about how we shouldn't be sitting on them because it makes the school look bad, everybody sits on them and nobody gets in trouble for it.

They hired this new math teacher that's crazy, but I think he's cool. He started writing all kinds of stuff on the board and I was like, *Yo, slow down and explain something, 'cause I'm lost as hot sauce.* Then the class laughed and he laughed, but he did slow down.

I sat there trying to figure out some math stuff when Ellie walked up and sat down next to me.

This okay, she said.

Free country, I said back. I don't really be talking to many peeps at Percy. I keep mostly to myself. Even though I play ball, I don't really be hanging with the ballplayers much either. When Miah was still living, me and him wasn't tight, but it wasn't nothing negative in it. He was different from me. I knew his dad was this famous film producer. And his moms was a writer. It was one of those whisper, whisper things you hear around, so I wasn't too sure until I looked up *Roselind* on the Internet. And there was a whole lot of stuff—even some old pictures of Miah at the Academy Awards. I was like, *Yo, this ain't your around the way, Brother!* And then after he died, all the stuff just started flying. I guess the cops thought it was just gonna be like, Oops, we made a mistake, but people went ballistic! Both those cops went to jail, and that's something you don't be seeing in New York—white cops going to jail for shooting a black kid—what?! Uh-uh. Most usually happens is they get desk duty until the hoopla dies down and then it's all back to how it was. The day those cops got sentenced, I swear, everybody in New York that was over the age of ten stood somewhere with their mouths hanging open. Then a whole lotta people started cheering.

Ellie was Miah's girl. They was real tight—he'd walk her to class. You'd see him in the hallway, carrying her books—sometimes she'd be carrying his books 'cause she believes in stuff like that, I guess—but still, Miah'd be looking like, *Yeah! She's mine.* It wasn't nothing snobby in it. They were in love and you could just tell it. I ain't gonna judge him. I mean, I wouldn't date no white girls, but it's just 'cause—well, for one thing, black girls got it going on, and me and my girl's tight. That interracial thing—you see it in movies and read it in books—everybody's doing that thing nowadays. But back in the day, brothers would get hung or get a serious beatdown for even looking at a white girl, so while I don't mean no disrespect to Miah, I'm not trying to forget the history. But I said *What's up?* to Ellie and she said *What's going on?* to me and we just sat there like that for a few, watching people go into the school.

"Pretty out," Ellie said.

"Yeah," I said back. "It's all right."

I took a look at Ellie's legs. Most of the girls wore their skirts real short, but hers was only kinda short and she had nice legs to go with it, even if they was mad pale.

"You're a junior this year?" Ellie asked me.

"Nah, I'm outta here. This my last year."

"You thinking about college and stuff?" Ellie looked at me. I'd never really sat this close to her. The closest I was to her was at Miah's funeral—and then I was a few rows back. I remember she wasn't crying. She sat up real straight and I remember thinking, *If somebody blinks too hard, that girl's gonna shatter like a bottle.* I tried to keep my eyes kinda open after that. Not 'cause I thought she was gonna break, really—I kept them open because I thought if *I* blinked too hard, I was gonna start crying and never be able to stop.

But now, sitting up close to Ellie, I could see that her hair wasn't just dark brown. It had some other kinds of brown in it. And when she looked at me, her eyes had some other colors in them too.

"Gonna go where the good ball teams are. That's my plan. The schools that got the good ball teams and a lotta money to shake at me. Got a couple I'm thinking about but I ain't said yes to anybody yet."

Ellie smiled.

"God, you sound just like Miah when you say—"

"You know how many times I heard that since Miah been dead?" I looked down at my backpack—too mad to look at her. "Twenty? Thirty? A hundred? Every time I turn around, somebody—and it usually ain't a black person—is saying something about me is reminding them of Miah."

"Why are you like this?" Ellie said, and I couldn't believe *she* had the nerve to be getting mad.

"Like what? Like me?"

"All angry . . . and evil." She moved her hands when she talked—like she was trying to draw who I was with those skinny pale arms.

"Guess black folks just angry people, huh? Try kicking it in my shoes, El. Some white girl dies who doesn't even look a little like you—only thing you got going on is you both white. And you one of maybe four white people at school with all black people." I looked at her, waiting for her to let what I was saying dig deep. "Say that other white girl eats some cop's bullet just 'cause she was the wrong color at the wrong time. And then people start coming out the woodwork trying to see that girl in you."

Ellie looked straight ahead and nodded.

"You know what you'd probably be thinking?" I asked then, kept going before she had a chance to answer. "You'd probably be thinking, 'Well, when the hell is MY number gonna be up?'"

"Is that what you think?"

I shrugged. "I think a whole lot of things and yeah, that's one of the thoughts. Another is—all these years gone past and white people still can't tell us apart."

"Kennedy, I was trying—"

"Doesn't matter. Think about it." A white guy passed and looked at us. When he was inside, I said, "Does *he* remind you of Miah?"

Ellie looked at me. "He doesn't play ball and he's not black—so no. And yes, I'm trying to see some Miah in you." She threw her arms out. "I'm trying to see some Miah in every single person I see—not just you. So if that makes me some kind of stupid racist, then I guess I'll be that if I get to see him a little. . . ."

I didn't say anything, just started getting my stuff together. Ellie kept looking straight ahead. Just staring.

"Yo, El. I know he was your man, and I know you guys was mad tight and all. I know it must've hurt. . . ."

"It still does," she said, real quiet.

I stood there with my backpack on my shoulder. Wasn't hardly anybody left on the stairs, and I wasn't looking to be late for math, but something kept me standing there.

"Look, El. I'm sorry I flashed on you. And I know I ain't never said this, but I'm sorry you lost your man. Miah was cool. The way I figure it, if it takes you a hundred years to get over it, then take the hundred years—it's just time, right? We all just doing our time on this planet anyways. Got a right to do it the way you need to."

Ellie looked at me for a minute. Then she nodded.

"Thanks, Kennedy."

I shrugged. "You don't have to be thanking me. I'm just telling you what's up."

I turned and started heading up the stairs. I could feel Ellie's eyes on me. And another pair of eyes too—I knew who they belonged to and I knew he was nodding and saying, *Yo, Kennedy. Thanks, man.*

Ellie

AT SCHOOL THERE WERE SIGNS EVERYWHERE—CHEERLEADING, debate team, track, soccer, chess club, reading group. I walked through the halls slowly, stopping to read each and every sign. *Come join us*, the signs seemed to beckon. *Why in God's name would anyone walk alone?*

It was true—there were kids everywhere—talking, calling to each other, sharing notes and lunch and stories about their weekends. When the bell rang, the halls got loud and busy. The sounds swirled around me and over me as I walked, as though there were some kind of invisible *thing* covering me, keeping me just that far away from everyone. How could anyone ever get it?

In the classrooms, the teachers looked at me with soft, sad eyes. In the cafeteria, I turned to catch kids whispering as they looked in my direction.

I answered questions when called on. I waved to people who waved to me. I carried my books close to my chest and walked the halls alone. The noise that was Percy Academy became muted and distant and foreign. Who were these people?

Miah died in the winter. Spring came with lots of rain. Then crocuses in patches at playgrounds, narcissus in silver pots on windows, tulips at Easter time. Then it was summer. Then it was fall again.

I remember a day with lots of snow and me not getting out of bed. I remember the morning I slammed my fist into the mirror—the glass, the bleeding, the wanting to die. But the cuts were not deep and the mirror was replaced. I remember screaming. Lots and lots of screaming. And a rage so deep, some days I couldn't stop shaking from it.

Somewhere inside of all of this, there was a funeral. There were rallies and news programs and politicians promising to protect young black men. There was a trial and two cops went to jail. Percy put up a plaque and the basketball team wore black bands around their arms.

And then there was less rage and a new hollowness. A pit of warm, dry air inside of me.

Then, for a long time, nothing at all.

Through it all, the seasons continued to change. Day

fell into night. My mother did chores. Dogs barked and car horns honked. Everywhere in the city, there were people who had no clue about the pain.

At school I took my tests. Did my homework. Each quarter, the A's on my report cards seemed to stumble over themselves. It was as if I was a grown-up coming back to school with all this new information. I had no friends. Everything and everyone seemed like it was part of a long-ago time—when I was young and free and living.

Desire Viola Roselind

ALL DAY LONG, THE CICADAS BEAT THEIR WINGS. THE SUN moves out from behind clouds and shines on your skin. I sit, fanning myself, a tall glass of lemonade always at my side. You want summer—it's summer. You want to watch the leaves change color, you move to another spot and you got yourself some autumn. Or maybe you feel like lying on the ground and making yourself a snow angel—just take some steps and you got yourself your own private winter. My grandson won't go near the snow. He says it reminds him of the night he fell. He won't say *died.*

I sit in my big chair and watch him watching the world some days. His body sags down and he lets himself get all wrapped up in a sadness just like his daddy used to do. I look at him and see Norman and Nelia and my own daddy—all coming through to him.

Jeremiah, you don't always got to be watching the

world, I say. I'm sitting in my spring with the cicadas singing. Jeremiah sitting in summer with the heat coming down and the sun so bright, the sky where he is is near white.

Jeremiah has a basketball. He can hold it in one hand. He can shoot it from way over there and it goes right into the basket. He can bounce it all kinds of ways that make you believe in magic. If he wants to play some basketball, all he's gotta do is get up and walk on over there and some boys who play really good will show up and they'll have themselves a good game. He gets the ball in the basket a whole lot of times. And he can do some fancy moves to take it away from one of the other boys.

That's when you see Jeremiah grinning.

But most days he just sits and watches the world. And that's when I try to talk to him.

You done left that world behind you, I say. *Let it go.*

But Jeremiah looks out on the world and shakes his head.

Can't let it go, Grandma. Got too many people missing me. Thinking about me. And I'm thinking about them too.

I look out at my flowers. The roses are red and pink and striped. Got roses with different-colored petals on the same flowers. Purple roses with color so deep, you choke up looking at them. Yellow-orange ones like little flames coming out of the green. Tulips too. And corn high as Jeremiah's head already and the spring still new. Got some rhubarb. Might bake a pie just to feel the crust forming against the palms of my hands. When my garden needs rain, it rains. Oh, if only living could've been like this.

If Jeremiah wanted, he could be in the front row of his favorite ball team's game. He could be swimming or eating ice cream. He could know what it feels like to fly. If he were a different kind of boy, he could stand in fire just because it was something he'd always wanted to do, or take steps down into the ocean and touch some shark's fin. Braid up the tentacles of a jellyfish.

But he's not that kind of boy. He's just a boy who can't let the world that he left behind get behind him.

I lean forward a little bit in my chair. I touch his head. Those twists he got is something I don't understand, but I still think his hair is beautiful. All of him is my beautiful Jeremiah. I let my hand run along his head and stare out to see what he's staring out at. There's his mama and daddy—Norman looking like he's putting on a little weight. I see Jeremiah's girl, Elisha, and her peoples. I see some animals, some little children, a ball game at Jeremiah's school. He's watching so many people and so many things.

One day, I say, *each of them is gonna be on this side with you. Seems like it's gonna take forever—*

I wish—

No you don't.

Jeremiah is sitting cross-legged at my feet. He's got the ball in his lap. Now he lowers his head until his forehead is touching it.

Yeah, Grandma. I do.

You left that world and it closed up behind you, Jeremiah. The way water do when a body climbs out of it. First there's some ripples and then the water gets all still again.

Jeremiah lifts his head up and lets himself smile a little. *The water's still rippling, though.*

I look out to where he's looking and I see he's telling the truth.

Ellie

NELIA WAS SITTING ON THE STOOP WHEN I GOT THERE EARLY
Saturday afternoon. She was wearing an orange T-shirt
and a beautiful tie-dyed skirt that wrapped around her
waist a couple of times and came all the way down to her
ankles. I walked down the block slowly, watching her as
she wrote in a black binder that covered a lot of her lap.
The block was quiet. At the other end, a group of girls
were playing hand games. I tried to listen to the song they
were singing, but they were singing so fast, the words
blurred together. Nelia'd gotten thin over the months. Her
face looked smaller, the cheekbones jumping up from it in
a way that was at once beautiful and alarming. I grabbed
the strap of my shoulder bag, needing something—anything—to hold on to. She would always be Miah's mom
to me.

"Hey, Nelia," I said when I was still a few feet away from her.

Nelia looked up, surprised. Then, slowly, she smiled. Miah's smile. I stood there for a moment, not able to take another step.

Then Nelia said, "I was hoping you'd stop by." And I felt myself melting, moving toward her like she was a life raft or something. We hugged and she held me tightly. I could feel her ribs beneath her shirt and skin, feel her still smiling.

"Sit down." She motioned to the stoop and I sat down one stair below her. For some reason the idea of sitting on the same step seemed too much. I needed to be able to look up at her.

"What are you working on? I mean—is it okay to ask that?"

Nelia gave me a puzzled look, then nodded. "Of course." She closed the binder. "I wish I could answer it, though—I don't really know. Just thoughts. Lots and lots of thoughts."

"Oh."

She touched my hair. Her hand felt so unfamiliar and so familiar at the same time.

"It's the way the books come to me. Thoughts are a good thing. A beginning."

Before I knew Miah, before I knew Nelia, I'd had to read a novel of hers for English class. It was about a black woman who was a civil rights attorney. She went back south to visit family and ended up in slavery. The teacher kept calling it magical realism, but there was nothing magical about it to me—It was one of the scariest, most impactful books I'd ever read. It haunted me for ages afterward. When the class discussed it, I couldn't even say anything and I remember the teacher asking if I had read it. It's strange. I'd read it the year before I'd met Miah. Then there he was in my life. Then there was Nelia Roselind, author of *And Back Again*. Who would have known they were heading toward my life? Who could have told me? What would I have believed? If someone had said, *You're going to meet the son of this author—a black guy, Ellie—you're going to fall in love with him and then he's going to die,* I would have backed away from that person. I would have given them such a look and called them crazy.

I leaned back against the step and stared up at the sky. Nelia and I were quiet for a while. It was beautiful out— the leaves were just beginning to change and there was only the slightest bit of wind, a strange wind, like someone stroking my shoulders.

Nelia put the binder down on the step beside her. It had

been a long time since she had written—I knew that. And I knew why too.

"It's been a long time," Nelia said. She smiled at me and I knew it was because my face showed everything. Surprise. Embarrassment. "You were just thinking that, weren't you?"

I nodded.

"Since Norman and I—"

"Broke up." I looked down at my fingers. "He left you—for Lois Ann King." The words came quickly. It felt like I had said them a thousand times. But I hadn't. Only heard it—again and again from Miah. *It busted my mama's heart wide open*, Miah used to say. *Hasn't written anything since.*

Nelia frowned. "Your life gets away from you," she said. "The older you get, the less of it you own."

I didn't understand what she was talking about, but she kept talking and it seemed that it didn't matter, right then, whether or not I was there.

"Even you knowing the whole story—whether I wanted you to or not—"

"I'm sorry—"

"No. It's not a secret anymore. We would've gotten close and eventually you would've known. But the fact that you knew the whole story before you even knew me—that part. That's your life not being your own any-more. It's funny. It's like writing a book—once it's out there, people say and do whatever they want with it. You have no control."

She looked at me, frowning still. "But who has control over *anything*, right?"

We were both quiet for a while. The sun went behind some clouds and everything got a bit darker for a moment. Then the sun came out again.

Nelia said, "It's hard to write when there's so much drama in your own life. Your own life gets in the way." She let out a long breath and looked down the block. The girls were still doing their hand-clapping thing and she watched them for a minute. "That's an old one—*Down, down, baby, down by the roller coaster, sweet, sweet baby, I'll never letcha go. Jimmy Jimmy coco-pop. Jimmy Jimmy pop!*"

I laughed. "Is that what they're saying?"

Nelia rolled her eyes. "Over and over and over. Someone needs to teach them something new. If they keep it up, it's going to be the title of this book. *Down, Down, Baby, Down by the Roller Coaster, Sweet, Sweet Baby, I Will Never Let You Go* by Nelia Roselind."

We laughed.

"And you'd probably get a Pulitzer for it."

"Oh, please, no. Who wants that much attention?"

"We read a book of yours in English Lit last year. And when I first got to Percy, we read *And Back Again*."

Nelia raised an eyebrow. "Really? I'd think that was a little young to be reading that book."

I shrugged. "It was for a Women's Lit class—I think it was mostly older kids taking the course. I thought the book was really beautiful—and really scary."

Nelia smiled. "I couldn't even imagine." She looked out over the block and shivered a little, then rubbed her hands over her arms. "When I'm writing, really in the heart of writing—it's like I'm not even there. Sarahbeth . . . you know, the main character . . ."

I nodded.

"She was so . . . so *foreign* to me. And every time something unexpected happened, I had to put my pen down . . . and shake it off. I couldn't *imagine* reading that book. Writing it was enough for me."

"But . . . I mean, then where does the stuff . . . the stuff you write about come from?"

Nelia shrugged. "I don't know really. I just write it down and ask no questions."

We looked at each other without saying anything. The girls had finally stopped singing and now there was piano music coming from one of the buildings across the street. Then, after a moment, a guy's voice, singing. I recognized the song—an old one by Fleetwood Mac. My sisters, who are both way older than me, used to listen to it all the time. It was a beautiful song about things changing.

"He has such a stunning voice," Nelia said.

We sat there listening awhile. The song made me think of so many things—of Anne and her girlfriend living in San Francisco. Of school and the kids who couldn't understand why the missing still hurt. Just last week, I'd overheard some girls talking in the hallway at school—maybe they had meant for me to hear, I don't know. *She's such a widow,* one of them said. *Give me a break, he was her boyfriend for less than a year. Get over it already.* I'd kept walking, ignoring them. Bounce back. Move on. Hide your tears. Get over it. That's how the world seemed to work. We get an hour to grieve, a few days off from school or work, then we're supposed to be right back in the world, as good as anything. I looked over toward the music and closed my eyes, blinking back the stupid tears that were welling up in them. That's why I was here—sitting on Nelia's stoop, close enough to touch her. I needed someone who understood that the hurting doesn't just stop, that the absence is so much bigger, so much more painful, so much more *present* than the presence was.

"Do you know who's singing?" I asked.

"That's Carlton. Miah's friend. You must have met him."

I smiled, remembering him. "I met him a few times. He was sweet. And funny."

We sat there, listening. His voice was amazing—soft and lilting. There was such a sadness to it. The Carlton I'd met hadn't had that sadness to him. But none of us did—not back then. Not before . . .

"You should go see him," Nelia said. "You're right—he is sweet." After a moment, almost to herself, she said, "Sweet and sad."

She picked up her binder again, opened it. "Number 434. Just ring the bell at the top of the stairs."

I stood up and she pointed across the street. "That brownstone over there. Follow the music." She smiled, then hugged me again, picked up her pen and leaned into the pages.

Jeremiah

WHEN I SIT DOWN BESIDE MY MOTHER, SHE SHIVERS. WHEN I touch Ellie's shoulders, she smiles like she knows it's me. Maybe she does. Who could have told me that the wind was some passed-on soul stopping to touch your face, your hands, your hair. Who knew a surprising cool breeze was someone who had gone before you, saying, "You're loved."

You're loved, Mama.

Ellie . . . you're loved.

Some days I wish hard for the chance to kiss Ellie again. But today—this moment—the two of them sitting on the stoop is perfect.

This is what I know now: In your life there will be perfect moments. And in your afterlife too.

My grandmother watches me and shakes her head. *Leave the living alone,* she says. But she doesn't understand. It's not easy to let go. Even if you turn your back on the world you left, you're still pulled toward it, you're still turning around—always—to look behind you. To make sure everyone's okay.

Carlton

SATURDAY MORNING, I WENT OVER TO A PICKUP GAME AT FORT Greene Park. I knew some of the brothers playing, but a bunch of them had come over from Bed-Stuy and Brownsville. One brother had on a Percy shirt. He had pretty good game, so I decided to ask him.

"What do you know about Percy?" I said.

He looked me up and down. Not in a mean way, but more in a *Who the hell is this light-skinned brother?* way. I'd seen the look a lot from darker-skinned brothers. It was a "chump until proven un-chump" look. I kept my gaze steady.

"What *you* know about it?" he asked back.

"I know they should have slammed Dalton in their final game last year, but didn't."

"True that." Then he let himself grin a little and held up his hand. I slapped it.

"Kennedy," he said. "I play ball there."

"Carlton. I'm over here at Tech."

The other guys were standing around the basket, tossing the ball around and taking shots. Me and Kennedy were standing midcourt. He was tall, about my height. I noticed right away that anytime he wasn't smiling, he was frowning.

Someone tossed him the ball and he took a shot— hardly even turning to look at the basket. The ball went in, though—nice and smooth too.

"I got Kennedy," I said. We were choosing up sides, and seeing his jump, I knew I wanted him on my team.

"I seen you play," Kennedy said. "You play a'ight." He smiled again. I looked back over to the other guys and picked another one. It went back and forth like that for a minute.

"You know Miah?" I asked Kennedy.

He'd bent down to pull up the tongue in his sneaks, but he stopped midpull and looked up at me. "Who ain't know Miah? After he got shot, everybody in New York claimed a piece of him."

"Yeah," I said.

Kennedy kept on looking at me. "He lived around here, didn't he?"

"On my block." I didn't look at him, just kept picking guys until each team had five players. "We went way back." After a minute I said, "Grew up together. Knew him since we were both five or six. He was my boy."

"So you really knew him—not just fronting like a lot of people."

"Yeah. We were pretty tight."

"The cops messed up. Nothing new, though," Kennedy said. "I didn't know him tight like you did, but he was always cool with me."

"Miah ain't all gone. He's still here."

Kennedy looked at me. And I looked back at him.

"You don't feel him?" I said.

He stared at me for another minute, then shrugged. "You know," he said. "Whatever."

"Check it," somebody said, and we started throwing the ball around. I took a shot and missed it. Kennedy retrieved the ball and chucked it back to me. We were just playing around, hadn't started a real game yet.

I dribbled the ball through my legs and behind my back, shot it and watched it sail in.

"Let's stop playing around and get this game on," one of the guys said.

I nodded. "Hit or miss, yo," I said.

Kennedy held his hands out. I threw him the ball and he took the shot, a sweet sinker. The game was on.

By the time I got home, it was late in the afternoon and I was sweaty and hungry as anything. The house was empty. My mom had cleaned and the hardwood floors smelled like the oil soap she used to clean them with. I made myself some lunch and ate it standing at the kitchen counter. I smelled bad and could feel myself stinking up my mother's clean kitchen, so I finished eating and went upstairs to take a shower. The whole time the water was washing away the funk, I was thinking about Kennedy—not only about the great game of ball he had going on, but also about the way he looked at me when I said that thing about Miah still being with us. There was something in that look that let me know that he felt it too. His look kept flashing in my head and then disappearing and replacing itself with how beautiful all those guys looked running up and down the court. I turned the water to cold, wanting to shut it all out. I didn't want to think about anything—not about Miah, not about Kennedy, not about the beautiful bodies of ballplayers . . .

After I got dressed, I went back downstairs and sat at the piano. The windows were wide-open—whenever my moms cleaned, she did that—like she was hoping the whole block could see what a clean house we had. I smiled and shook my head, not bothering to close them. That song "Landslide" had come to me again—all the words—and I tapped a few keys, ready to play it. I sang the song softly at first, letting the words move through me. I could feel myself beginning to sing louder and louder, wanting to forget, to sing right over the part of the day that made me feel ashamed—thinking about those beautiful bodies. And remember the good stuff—scoring, Kennedy's look, our team winning by ten points. Maybe I had sung the song twice or three times when the doorbell rang.

I waited a minute, hoping whoever it was would go away. But they didn't. The bell rang again and I figured I might as well answer it.

At first I didn't know who she was. She'd changed over the months. Her hair was longer and her clothes seemed—different. Then I remembered I'd only seen her out of her uniform once and that was at Miah's funeral. That day, she was dressed in black like everyone else. But this time, she was wearing jeans—the kind that fit low on the hips in a way that looked nice on her. She looked paler than I remembered. For some reason I'd remembered her as being the same complexion as my mom, but she wasn't. Her skin was whiter. The kind of skin that burned right up in the sun. Then she smiled. And I remembered that smile, remembered the way Miah always grinned when he talked about it.

"Hey, Ellie," I said.

She looked surprised. Then her smile got bigger. "So you remember me?"

I stepped back and let her in. "How am I gonna forget the love of my best friend's life?"

Ellie looked at me. "Is that what he called me?"

"He called you a lot of things."

"I heard you singing."

"Yeah. I sing."

We stood in the foyer a minute without saying anything, just sort of looking at each other. It was starting to get dark out and the inside of the house seemed too dark.

"I was visiting Nelia," Ellie said. "She showed me where you lived. Thought I'd, you know, stop by and say hey."

"Hey yourself. It's nice to see you." I put my hands in my pockets, then took them out again. "Come in," I said, backing up a bit. "You want some water or juice or something?"

Ellie shook her head, looking around as she walked, taking everything in, I guess. Our house was full of art that my dad collected—African masks, drums, oil paintings, things like that. She walked over to the couch and sat on the edge of it.

"It's pretty here."

"Yeah," I said. "It's a nice place. Lived here most of my life. You're uptown, right?"

She nodded. "Central Park West. An apartment—not a house. Brooklyn makes me wish we lived in a house, though. So much more air."

"Sometimes it's a lot of hot air, though. People hanging out, talking junk. I love Brooklyn, though. It's home to me."

We got quiet again. I didn't have any idea what else to say to her. She was Miah's girl and now Miah was gone. In some fairy-tale type novel, she'd probably end up being my girl, but this wasn't that kind of story. She was pretty enough and all, though. Maybe Kennedy . . .

"Hey—do you know this guy Kennedy? He goes to your school?"

A small frown, and then she said, "Yeah—I know him somewhat. He's not very friendly."

"It's New York," I said. "Who is?"

She nodded. "That's true. How come you ask? You know him?"

"He was over this way, playing ball in the park today. He's got good game. That was the first time I met him, though. Miah'd talked about his game a couple of times and I'd seen him play."

Ellie nodded. "He's supposed to be pretty smart too. I tried to talk to him a couple of times, but—he pretty much brushed me off." She shrugged. "I think it was my fault, though. I said something about him sounding like Miah. Sounds like, from what he said, he hears that a lot."

"You know how people are. He was probably getting

compared to Miah right and left. Especially at a place like Percy."

"Yeah. He kind of suggested that was the case." She looked across the living room. The windows go from the ceiling to the floor almost. I watched her staring out at the block. It was almost dark now. "I don't know. I was just trying to make conversation."

I got up and went into the kitchen and took two bottles of water from the fridge, then came back and tossed one to her. "Why?"

"Why what?"

"Why *try* to make conversation . . . why *try* to make it with Kennedy? Either convo happens or it doesn't."

Ellie opened the bottle of water and took a sip. "To connect. To remember. To forget. All of the above. Wrong reasons and right reasons."

"Yeah, I hear you. I get it."

"You know . . . ," Ellie said softly, "I feel like the world stopped. And I got off . . . and then it started spinning again, but too fast for me to hop back on. I feel like I'm still trying to get a . . . to get some kind of foothold on living."

I raised an eyebrow. "That's deep."

"You don't feel that way? I mean—you guys were best friends."

"Yeah. But for me, it's like there's this place where

there's just . . . nothing. Like this hole or something. I throw some TV or a movie or a book in it every now and then. I throw a lot of ball in there, and music—you know, I take steps. Press on."

Ellie stared out the window, then sighed and leaned back into the couch. "I guess that's what we're doing, huh? Guess we're pressing on."

"Yep."

"No girlfriend, huh?"

"Nope."

She looked at me. Then without blinking she said, "Boyfriend?"

"Nah. Just me. Just me trying to figure it all out." It felt like something heavy lifted up off of me. I took a breath and the breath came easily. Ellie hadn't even *blinked*.

"I think the figuring out takes forever," she said. "It seems like everybody's trying to figure something out."

"How about you—what's your thing? The thing you're trying to figure out? I mean, besides how to hop back onto the world."

Ellie shrugged. "I don't know, really—I mean, I guess that's the thing. How do we go on? How do we get back on the world and move along?"

"Well . . ." I sat down on the couch beside her. "I guess this is a step, huh? You ringing my bell."

Ellie smiled again. "I guess."

"It's a big day for me," I said.

" 'Cause I rang your bell?"

I took another sip of water. She hadn't even *blinked* when she asked about a boyfriend. And here I was thinking there'd be the world exploding out from under me.

"Yeah," I said. "Glad you crossed that street and rang my bell."

"Well, then I guess I'll have to do it again sometime."

"You better."

"And maybe one day you can cross that bridge to Manhattan."

"Maybe—it's a long bridge."

Ellie nudged me with her shoulder and smiled. I nudged her back.

"Nah, really, though," I said. "Thanks."

"Don't thank me. Nelia's the one who pointed your house out and suggested I come say hi. I just followed the music."

I started singing the song again. Ellie listened and after a moment she joined in—her voice high and soft in a way that blended nicely. I was surprised she knew the words, but didn't stop to ask her about it.

"And I saw my reflection . . . "

When the song ended, we sat there drinking our water and staring outside. It grew dark, but I didn't turn on any lights. Somewhere someone was playing a Stevie Wonder tune. Somewhere else, a little kid was singing her ABC's. Then the block got quiet. And another day was almost over.

Kennedy

SUNDAY, MY MOMS WAKES ME UP EARLY AND I TAKE A SHOWER, grease my braids a little and put on some decent clothes. She's already dressed, wearing dark blue, her black coat and pocketbook on the couch next to her Bible.

"Made you some bacon and eggs," she says when I come out of the bathroom. She sets the plate down on the kitchen table and smiles at me. "Don't you look nice."

I smile back, sit down and say, "So do you."

Sunday mornings, I miss my dad the most. His chair across from mine is empty. In our building some of the kids got dads and some don't. Some of them never met their dads and some see them on weekends.

Sunday mornings, we go to church and then go see my dad.

The whole time the preacher's preaching, I'm thinking about my dad. If anybody asked, I'd say he was good—like in his heart, he was good. You'd see him coming down the street and he was always carrying some lady's bag or helping somebody with one of their kids or giving some poor chump some spare change. That's the kind of guy I remember him being—somebody who was always thinking about other people. I guess somebody like that should have gone out real tragic—like, shot or something—like Miah. But he didn't. He went out early because he had a whacked heart. Something from when he was young that just stayed on and caught him when he was thirty-seven. Makes you always think about how you're living.

Even though it's freezing, the cemetery is hopping. Sunday seems to be Visit the Dead Day—people walking slowly up and down the rows and rows of dead people or crouching all close around some tiny grave. Makes a body wonder if the dead know what Sunday is and get all ready.

My daddy's grave is in a lot about a quarter mile in then another twenty feet to the left. KENNEDY MAYARD SR. it says. Something about the way his name looks there makes me wish gravestones wasn't stone—it seems real permanent that way. Like it's saying, *You better believe he's dead!*

I make a fist and pound it against my heart a couple of times, then throw the peace sign at him. My moms fixes the plastic flowers around the gravestone. We stand there a little while without saying anything. Then I'm feeling my dad right there with us—his arm around my mom's shoulder, his big hand rubbing my head.

My moms pulls her coat tighter and says, "Sure is windy today, isn't it?"

I look out over the cemetery. Even though it's only the third day of November, I see the first few flakes of snow.

Me and my moms stand there watching it come down—all soft and slow and cold.

It's strange the way death connects people. I wasn't real tight with Miah when he was living, but now here I was, standing in a brick-cold cemetery, feeling my dad everywhere and knowing that me and Ellie and Miah's moms and pops and everybody who'd ever lost somebody they'd been tight with—we all . . . it was like, I don't know—like a continuum—and we're all a part of the same something. We ate our breakfast and did our work and had conversations that were stupid and conversations that weren't so stupid. At night we closed our eyes and hoped sleep came quickfast. And with all of our living going on, our dead peeps were there—everywhere. Watching over us, holding us up, giving us some kinda reasons for going to church and school and the basketball courts. Always right there, making sure we kept on keeping on. I guess if anybody asked, I'd tell them we were all doing what the living do.

I take my mom's hand, pull her a little bit closer to me. She smells like cold weather and perfume.

"Your daddy always liked himself some snow," my moms says.

And we stand there, freezing our behinds off and watching it fall.

Norman Roselind

WHEN I FIRST MOVED TO FORT GREENE, WHAT I LOVED MOST were the trees. The city had planted saplings back in the sixties and now the trees stand like soldiers up and down the block. As though they're guarding the residents of Fort Greene from harm. I wish I could say they do. It amazes me that they're still standing—that anyone or anything is still standing. The trees change—leaves bud, grow green and wide, wither, turn red and brown, then fall. Again and again. Year after year. When Miah was a little boy, he'd climb up and swing on the lowest branches and invariably, some adult would lean out of a window and say, "Miah, get down off of that tree and let it grow like you grow." For some reason, that always made Miah laugh—the idea of a tree having the same upward journey as himself.

Some mornings, I sit on my stoop and look at the *Times,* see the way the world is stopping and the way it just keeps moving on. Amazing how it keeps moving on. Amazing how people can melt themselves into each new day.

This morning, Nelia was sitting across the street on her stoop. Used to be our stoop.

The wind was blowing hard. It'd been cold last night and the day felt like it was trying to warm up but not doing a good job at it. Nelia was leaning over her writing. Her hair was getting longer and it sort of fell down a bit over her face in a way I'd never seen it do. Miah's death had added some years to her and thinned her up. At some angles she looked like the Vassar girl I'd fallen in love with years and years ago. Then she looked like an older, more beautiful version of the woman I'd walked away from. I closed my eyes. Miah'd never understood how two people could stop loving each other and I'd never known how to explain.

After a while of watching Nelia, I took a deep breath, folded the paper under my arm, got up from my stoop and crossed the street.

How many years had it been since I'd crossed that street—three, four, nine? Even after Miah died, I still didn't go back into that house. I'd offered to help clean out his room, but Nelia had said no, said she'd take care of it. Now here were my feet, one stepping in front of the other, and me moving closer and closer to Nelia's stoop.

The block is silent as a stone. It feels like somebody far away is watching. And waiting to see what happens.

Ellie

EARLY SATURDAY MORNING, MARION SHAKES ME AWAKE. MY
throat hurts and I'm not sure where I am.

"You were screaming," she says.

I blink, look around my room.

"Someone shot Miah," I whisper, pressing my hand to
my throat. "I dreamed someone shot Miah."

Marion stares at me and shakes her head. She leaves
and a few minutes later, she's back, pressing a warm cloth
to my forehead.

"I dreamed . . ."

"Shhhh, Elisha," she whispers. "Miah's gone, honey."

I lay back on the bed and close my eyes. "Miah's gone,"
I whisper, sinking back into sleep.

When I came downstairs later, I was surprised to find my
father sitting at the kitchen table. The apartment smelled

like cinnamon, apples and coffee. Marion gave me a long look, then put a glass of juice on the table in front of me.

"What are you doing home?" I asked my father. He was usually at the hospital on Saturdays. Sundays were our day together.

"Your mother tells me you had another bad dream," my father said. He looked tired, his blue eyes were rimmed and puffy. My sisters and brother call me "the accident" because I was born ten years after the last one. My parents aren't young. Last year, we celebrated my mother's fifty-seventh birthday.

I looked at Marion. "And?"

"And we're worried," she said. "It's been almost a year now, Elisha."

"It's been eleven months, *Marion*."

"Don't call your mother 'Marion,' El."

I pushed the juice away from me. "When she starts calling me 'Ellie,' I'll start calling her 'Mom'—"

"Your name is Elisha." Marion turned back to the stove and stirred something. After a moment, she set a bowl of apple compote on the table, then took a stack of pancakes from the oven.

I got up and poured myself some coffee.

"We're just concerned," my father said. "You don't participate in school—"

"I get straight A's." I tried to keep my voice even.

96

"You don't do any activities, just study, study, study," Marion said. She sat across from me and put two pancakes on a plate. "Here."

"Not hungry."

My father looked at me and I rolled my eyes and took the plate from Marion.

"No sports, no clubs, no friends . . . ," Marion said, counting off on her fingers. "Just bad dreams and sadness. Just you in your room, doing I don't know what. . . ."

"*Studying*. I'm *studying* in my room. And I do other stuff besides hang out upstairs."

"Like what?" Marion and my father looked at me. "Where are your friends? Girls your age are supposed to have lots of girlfriends hanging around and calling. Nobody ever calls here for you. When the other kids were home, the phone was constantly—"

"Well, I'm not *the other kids*. You should have stopped when you were ahead if you wanted *the other kids*."

"We were thinking," my father said, "that maybe you want to talk to somebody—"

I started to say something, but he put his hand up.

"I know we've talked about it before, but now all this time has passed and you're the same."

I'm not the same, I wanted to scream. *I'm different. My boyfriend was killed. That does something to a person.*

"Sometimes I go to Brooklyn and visit Miah's mother

and Carlton," I said. I knew I couldn't make them understand, and I knew some psychiatrist friend of my father's wouldn't understand either.

"When are you taking all these trips to Brooklyn?" Marion asked.

"Just sometimes." I took a bite of pancake and chewed slowly.

Both of them waited.

"Who's Carlton?" Marion wanted to know.

I looked up at the clock over the kitchen sink. It was almost nine thirty. Carlton and I had said we'd meet downtown at eleven for brunch.

"He was Miah's best friend."

My mother put her fork down on the table. "And now you're dating *him*?"

"God—can't you guys leave me alone? I'm not *dating* him."

"What's going on, Ellie?" my father said. "What's this about? There're plenty of boys living right around you. Nice boys."

"You mean *white* boys, Dad."

"I mean more appropriate boys." My father looked at me and I looked back at him without saying anything. I'd always loved him more than my mother and maybe that's why it hurt to hear him talk like that.

"Give me a break, Dad. Cut the liberal crap. You mean white boys, but you would never say that, because it would be politically incorrect, wouldn't it?"

My father shook his head and stared at me like he was trying to figure out who I was.

Marion got up and went over to the sink. She stood there with her back to us as though she'd forgotten what she'd gone there for.

"Maybe it's a good thing, honey. Maybe it means less sadness in the house."

"I don't understand you," my father said. "I thought I did, but I don't."

"I understand *you* even less," I said. "And I'm not dating him. He's . . . he's a friend."

"Well," Marion said. "It's good to hear you're making some friends. I don't want you going all the way to Brooklyn, though."

"I'm meeting him downtown today." I took another bite of pancake. "Don't worry—I won't be crossing that dangerous bridge into an outer borough."

"Don't be sarcastic," my father said. "I still think we need to talk about you seeing someone."

I stood up. "How about family therapy? I'm game for that. How about I get a chance to talk about why I was too scared to bring my black boyfriend home to parents who swear they're not racist. How about we talk about him dying without you ever meeting him because somewhere along the way, I got the message that it wasn't okay—"

"Bring this new friend home," Marion said. "No one's stopping you."

I didn't take my eyes off my father. "That's not the point, is it?"

"It's all something we need to talk about," he said.

I shook my head. "We never will," I said.

My parents were silent. They knew it was true.

Carlton

"IT'S FUNNY. THERE'S THIS PART OF ME THAT ALWAYS KINDA felt alone, you know?"

We're in a coffee shop on the corner of Waverly and Sixth Avenue. There are people all around us—men and men together, women and men, parents and kids, women and women.

"I used to come here with Miah," Ellie said, leading me to a table in the back. We sat down and a waiter put two menus in front of us. The place was quieter than it seemed it ought to be. I looked up and saw that the ceilings were covered with a purple foamy material that must have absorbed a lot of the sound.

"How'd you guys find it—I mean, I come to the Village a lot and I never even noticed this place."

Ellie looked at me. "We were walking once. God, it all feels like such a long time ago. And we passed this couple—interracial—older, like in their thirties or something. And the guy says to Miah, 'Yo, take your honey . . .' and he told us about this place. We just smiled. It was like this bonding moment or something. And then we came here. All kinds of people mixed up all kinds of ways. Black, white, gay, straight. It doesn't make any kind of difference here."

I looked around, nodding. It was easy to imagine Miah here with Ellie, the two of them at a quiet table, drinking cappuccinos and talking about their lives. Nobody looking at them, judging them, hating them just because . . .

I stared down at the menu, my eyes starting to burn. Maybe it was the big memory of Miah. Maybe it was thinking about how good that must have felt, to be out and open and not caring about the rest of the world. When the waiter returned, we both ordered and I started messing with a napkin, tearing it into tiny pieces. I couldn't look at Ellie for some reason. The word *gay* seemed so loud, so everywhere at once.

"Something about coming here," Ellie said. "It made me so sure of Miah. So sure that I loved him. That everything would be okay." Her voice cracked a bit and she got quiet again.

Outside, snow was blowing—not a whole lot, and it probably wouldn't stick, but enough to let us know that winter was definitely here.

"You're lucky," I said. "I mean, to have had a chance to feel so sure about something. There's not one single part of me I've ever been a hundred percent sure about."

"Hmmm." Ellie looked at me. "Nothing?"

"Ball, I guess. I wasn't always sure of my game, but I always loved playing ball." I opened my palm and stared at it. "The way the ball feels in my hand. The way a shot slides into a basket. Running full court and getting underneath the backboard in time—all of that's always felt . . . felt real. Solid. But show me a ballplayer that's out there going pro saying, 'My boyfriend Bob and me . . .' "

Ellie smiled. Our food came.

"Don't exist," I said after the waiter left. "I don't exist."

"I thought you said you didn't have a boyfriend?" Ellie looked at me, frowning.

"I *don't*. That's what I'm saying. I don't exist—gay ballplayers don't exist."

"That's crazy, Carlton. You're going to stop being who you are because—"

"Yep."

"But that's not . . . that's not *living*."

"I know."

"And just because people aren't *out*, doesn't mean they don't exist."

I didn't say anything. If someone had said to me, *Carlton, are you straight or gay? Tell me now because you might be dead tomorrow,* I would say, *I'm gay*—even though I've never kissed another guy or been in love with anybody.

"I *am* gay," I said, not looking at Ellie. I watched the syrup sink into my pancakes, watched the way the orange slices beside the pancakes lay still as glass.

"I know," Ellie said.

When I looked up, she was smiling again.

We stared at each other for a long time. I felt myself choking up. Felt like Ellie had just saved my life somehow. I wanted to holler, to reach across the table and lift her up. But my breath was coming too fast and my body felt heavy and light all at once, so I just sat there, staring at her.

"We'd make a nice couple—aesthetically, don't you think?" Ellie said.

I laughed and the air felt the tiniest bit lighter.

"Seriously, Carlton. You're beautiful—you could have guys dropping for you all over the place."

I took a bite of my pancakes, shook my head.

"I think I'm some kind of romantic. I would love to fall in love and feel like that's it—that's the be-all, end-all, forever amen."

Ellie's fork froze. When she looked at me, I don't know if I was surprised to see her eyes were watery. She blinked but didn't say anything.

"I know that's what you guys had," I said quickly.

"I just wonder . . . you know—if you can have it more than once. I mean, I'm not looking and I don't know if I'll ever be looking. I wasn't even looking when I found Miah." She laughed. "But . . . who knows. Who knows anything."

"I can't even imagine your world."

Ellie smiled.

"Yeah," she said. "That's what I like—you don't even try to."

"Miah loved you like crazy—you know that, right?"

Ellie stared down at her plate and nodded. "Most days," she said.

"All days."

"Most days I know it was all days. But some days . . ." She looked up at me and laughed a little bit. "Some days, I think—"

"Well, those days you're wrong."

"I know. I mean, most of me knows."

"Your food's getting cold."

She started eating. I watched her for a while.

"It never even crossed my mind to go uptown and see you," I said. "But I'm sure as hell glad you crossed that street."

"Like I said before, don't thank me—thank Nelia."

I started eating again. "You. Nelia. Whoever. I'm glad it happened."

"Yeah." Ellie looked over at me and smiled. Miah was right—it was one of the prettiest smiles I'd ever seen—real, deep, sincere, like her face and heart were wide-open.

"You want to catch a movie later?"

Ellie nodded. "Definitely."

"We'll get the paper and see what's playing, cool?"

"Way cool with me."

It was Saturday morning still. The rest of the day was ours. The rest of our life was ours. Winter was coming and it was cold outside. But we were sitting inside a restaurant that was quiet and warm. The food was good. The company was good. Maybe one day I'd have myself someone to be in love with. But even if I didn't right now, the world was ours. And here me and Ellie were, sitting across from each other. Smiling.

Kennedy

IN THE SECOND QUARTER, TRINITY SNATCHES THE BALL FROM our weak point guard—who should be sitting on the bench, but isn't because his daddy gives big money to Percy—and scores. I curse and the ref calls a foul on me because you ain't supposed to be cursing on the court. Our team's down by ten points and looking to lose yet another game. It's my third foul, so the coach pulls me off the floor. I curse again, but not so anybody can hear it, take the bench, feeling the sweat rolling off me, and put the towel over my head so I can't see how bad we're doing.

"Gotta learn to watch that mouth, Kennedy," the coach says to me.

"Yeah, whatever," I say from under the towel.

"And that attitude."

I don't say *whatever* again, but I'm thinking it hard enough for the whole gym to feel it. It's full tonight because this game is only the fourth one in the season and even though we already lost the first two out of three, people still feeling hopeful about Percy. I hear the crowd cheering and look out from underneath my towel to see Percy score from midcourt. Even more surprised to see that it's our weak point guard actually doing something for the team.

The game goes back and forth for a while and I don't look at the coach because I don't want him to see how much I'm hurting to get back in the game.

"Keep yourself warm," Coach says, throwing me my sweats. "No use cramping up."

I pull the sweats on. Percy scores two more baskets and then gets fouled. After a while the score's tied.

"Go on out," Coach says to me. He pulls the point guard out and we slap hands on the way on and off the court. His hand is sweaty and he's got this big grin on his face like he's done a whole lot.

The crowd starts cheering when they see I'm back. Since Miah's been gone, I'm the big scorer on the team. He'd get out here and pull down twenty, thirty, sometimes even forty points a game. Most games, I go home with about twenty. Coach says if my attitude was a little better, I'd probably pull down a whole lot more.

It's Percy's ball and the forward shoots it my way. I

take it up court and slip a layout in easily. The crowd starts going crazy, cheering and stomping and whistling. Even though I'm still bent about that foul, I feel myself starting to grin. I flip the crowd a peace sign and they go even crazier.

We score a few more baskets and then even *I'm* feeling the love in the room. I look over at Coach and he's got this big smile on his face. Like he's thinking what I'm thinking—*Hey, y'all—we're the Percy Panthers. And we're BACK!*

Outside, there's like a trillion stars in the sky and the night's colder than anything. I pull my hood over my head and lift my knapsack higher on my shoulder, ready to make a quick trek to the subway, when I hear somebody calling my name. I turn and see Ellie coming up to me— Ellie and Carlton.

I give Carlton a look as I slap his hand. We hug real quick. I'm feeling good, so I even give Ellie a quick hug.

"You went *off*," Carlton says to me.

"Forty-two points, yo!" We slap hands again, both of us grinning. "Most I ever scored in one game."

"You keep going like that—"

"Yeah," I say before he can even finish. "Put Percy on the map finally. How's Tech doing?"

"We doing okay," Carlton says.

"They're doing more than okay," Ellie says. "Won their last four games."

I look from one to the other, then back again, and raise my eyebrows.

Carlton smiles. "Nah, man," he says. "It's not like that. We're friends."

Ellie looks confused for a minute, then she smiles.

"Oh," I say. "That's what they calling it these days."

People start pouring out of Percy, moving around us, slapping my hand and telling me what a good game I had.

"Yo—thanks for coming, but I gotta get out of this cold."

Ellie looks at me. "Maybe you can come and get a bite with us or something. We're going to the diner around the corner. Nothing big."

Carlton starts jumping up and down, his hands in his pockets. "You know—a little warm-up before we head across that bridge."

"Nah, man," I say. "I'm not into that third-wheel thing. You know how 'friends' be acting."

Ellie rolls her eyes. "It's not like that, Kennedy."

"True that," Carlton says, grinning. "I'm gay, man. Can you handle that?"

I look at him, then take a step back. "Hey, it ain't nothing. You know. It takes all kinds and all." Then after a minute, I say, "Damn. For real, man?"

Carlton nods. "And no offense, Kennedy, but you're not my type."

I stand there a minute, trying to let stuff sink in.

"I mean, it don't mean anything to me, but—like, for real, *gay*?"

Carlton just looks at me.

"Damn," I say again. "Whatever. That's *your* thing." Then it hits me. "Yo! Were you and Miah like . . . together—"

"Kennedy!" Ellie says. But she's smiling. "C'mon. I was the one with Miah, remember? Hello?"

I shrug. "You know. Sometimes brothers go both—"

"Don't even," Ellie says.

Carlton shakes his head. "Nah, man," he says. "Me and Miah were friends. Believe it or not, straight guys and gay guys can hang without it being a thing."

"I know that. What—you think you're the first gay boy I ever talked to or something?"

Carlton just kinda smiles. "How would I know? We're just getting to know each other."

"Well, you're not. I don't live under some rock or something. I've seen some things." I thought about all the

111

gay brothers at my church—*I* knew they were gay whether they were calling it that or not. And my uncle James is gay—and not scared to tell anybody.

"Anyway," Ellie says. "Tonight is . . ." She hugs herself and looks around a bit. "You know, the night Miah died."

I feel the wind leave me a little bit. I feel myself starting to sweat, even in the cold.

None of us says anything. People keep moving around us and I hear *Good game, Kennedy* again and again, but the words sound like they're coming from far away. I hear myself cursing again.

"You coming?" Carlton asks.

"Yeah, let's at least go get some fries or something," I say. "Show a dead brother some love."

"That dead brother probably helped you get that ball in the basket all those times," Carlton says.

"Well, I'm all for that." I give Carlton another look. I want to say, *The way you play ball, man—you sure you're gay?* But I'd had enough with that conversation for one night.

Carlton puts his arm around Ellie's shoulder.

"It's like *crazy* stars out tonight," he says.

And me and Ellie and him look up. And keep on looking.

Nelia

WINTER NOW. I TRY NOT TO MARK THE DAYS. HE GOT SHOT on a Saturday in December. We buried him that Monday. I closed the date book on my writing desk a long time ago. Over a year has passed since Miah died. The date book is black with gold letters on the front—*Remember*, it says. And I do.

It's snowing this morning. I stand at the window and watch the white flakes come down, sprinkle themselves over the block like someone's chenille bedspread. I eat a fried egg sandwich standing, look up at the silvered sky.

And remember.

The first third of my book is done now. There is a little girl telling the story—a ghost named Annabelle. Do I believe in ghosts? Now I do. Annabelle walks through this house and across my pages and tells her story. I listen and write it down—and in her story are the stories of people

I've known and people I hope to meet one day. One day someone will read this book and maybe it will make them laugh. Or cry. Who knows. All I know is what I have here—a third of a finished book, a girl named Annabelle, black print on white paper, a new world to walk into.

The writing comes to me and I let it. Some days it is so filled with sadness that I have to lie down, sleep, forget for a while. Some days there is an absolute joy to it.

Some days there is Ellie in my kitchen, the yellow-gold light spilling over us as we talk. Some evenings there is Norman on my stoop, telling me about his life, listening to me talk about mine—friends now, the past of us together not as painful as it once was. And on Saturdays there is Carlton, carrying my grocery bags—when I say, *Sing, Carlton,* he does, and his soft voice takes me back to another time, a lighter time, a freer time.

And each day there is at least one perfect moment—the way the sun moves around the living room, roasted potatoes with lots of rosemary and oil, a new baby wrapped up in blue, a child laughing.

The snow blows and blows. I turn away from my window, make my way upstairs to my study. When I turn my lamp on, so much beautiful light fills the room.

Ellie

WHAT SURPRISES ME STILL IS HOW MUCH DOESN'T CHANGE. You go outside and the night sky is still night sky—moon waxing and waning, stars—some brighter than others. Day means clouds or no clouds, rain or no rain. Cold or hot. You sweat. You cry. You walk and eat and pull your socks up when they fall down. You lace up your boots or strap on your sandals. You walk into a store and buy a new shirt. A day or two later you wear it and somebody says, *Hey, nice shirt. Is it new?*

You go days without remembering and then for days you can't forget. But your smile comes more often. And the world seems to open its arms to you.

You laugh with Carlton. You have long, deep conversations with Nelia, you begin to talk more with Kennedy—whose smile, when it comes, is like a small gift.

You sit some mornings and think about what those

who leave us leave behind—this . . . this potential for a new life . . . a different life. This *gift* of a future that we never imagined, filled with people we might have otherwise overlooked.

This morning there is so much snow on the ground. I walk slowly to Central Park. When I get to the entrance, I feel my heart start to beat hard. But I keep walking. The park is empty and still. The branches dip down with the weight of the snow.

Then I get to the place where Miah fell and wait for my screaming to come. But it doesn't. Instead the wind lifts up, blowing my hair into my eyes. Blowing the snow up around me. I listen to the sound it makes. *Shhhh. Shhhh. Shhhh.*

"Jeremiah Roselind," I whisper. "I will *always* remember you."

The wind takes my words, lifts them gently into the air.

"Always," I say again.

And the wind moves softly across my cheeks. Tender as a hand.

Jeremiah

ELLIE EISEN. I WILL ALWAYS REMEMBER YOU.

When you die, you turn away from the world you've always known and begin the long, slow walk into the next place. And behind you—everyone you left is taking a step deeper into their new world. The world they're learning to live in without you.

When you die, your voice becomes the wind and whispers to the living—

Ellie. You're loved.

Carlton. You're loved.

Mama. You're loved.

Pops. You're loved.

And Kennedy—hey, Kennedy—you got game, yo!

And when each of the people you left behind has heard,

you turn slowly and begin your long walk into *your* new world.

But some every now and then you stop, look behind you.

And remember.

IN HER OWN WORDS

Jacqueline Woodson Shares Some Thoughts and Insights About
If You Come Softly

Where it takes place:
In the Washington Heights section of Manhattan.

Where I wrote it:
Whidbey Island, which is off the coast of Seattle, Washington, and in Olivebridge, New York.

Why I wrote it:
I wrote *If You Come Softly* because I wanted to write about first love—how hard it can be and how great it is. I also wanted to write about being fifteen because I remember that age very well. As I was writing it, I came across some lines from Romeo and Juliet. The enemies to Jeremiah and Ellie's love are racism, police brutality, and people's general stupidity. I also wanted to write about Time—about how fleeting it is, how important it is to love who you want and be who you want in the moment so that you don't look back and think, "I should have . . ." or "I could have . . ."

JACQUELINE WOODSON SHARES SOME THOUGHTS AND INSIGHTS ABOUT

Behind You

WHERE IT TAKES PLACE:

Fort Greene, Brooklyn, and Manhattan's Upper West Side.

WHERE I WROTE IT:

At home in Brooklyn and in Manhattan.

WHY I WROTE IT:

I had written a book called *If You Come Softly*. Once I finished that book, the characters still haunted me. Then 9/11 happened and I was faced with trying to figure out how we move on when we lose people so suddenly. I started thinking about it all and this book began.

Jacqueline Woodson shares some thoughts and insights about herself

What's your favorite color?
Blue, sometimes green but mostly blue.

What's your favorite food?
Pizza.

What foods don't you like?
Avocado, mushrooms, artichokes, raspberries, papaya, meat, brussels sprouts, alfalfa sprouts, oatmeal . . . This list is actually much longer, but I'll stop here.

Do you have brothers and sisters?
I have an older brother and an older sister and a younger brother. Even though I'm five feet ten inches tall, I'm the shortest person in my family.

Where were you born?
Columbus, Ohio, but I spent my early life in Greenville, South Carolina. We moved to Brooklyn when I was about seven.

What was your favorite subject in school?
I loved English and anything where we got to do writing. I was terrible at math and science. I loved gym and Spanish and anything that allowed us to dance or jump around. I wasn't a big fan of sitting still too long unless I was reading. I always read the same books again and again.

WHAT ARE/WERE SOME OF YOUR FAVORITE BOOKS?

As a kid, I loved anything by Virginia Hamilton or Judy Blume. I also loved *The Selfish Giant* by Oscar Wilde and *The Little Match Girl* by Hans Christian Andersen. Oh—and *Stevie* by John Steptoe. These days, I feel like my favorites list grows and grows. A sampling of the authors and illustrators I love: Chris Raschka, Chris Lynch, Chris Myers—and not because they all have the same name! I also love An Na, Karen Hesse, Kashmira Sheth, Mildred Taylor, James Baldwin, Anne Lamott, Rosa Guy, Christopher Paul Curtis, Walter Dean Myers, Hope Anita Smith, Carson McCullers, Raymond Carver, Audre Lorde. . . . I could go on and on.

WHY DO YOU LOVE WRITING SO MUCH?

Because it makes me happy. Even when the words are slow in coming and the story seems all lopsided, writing keeps me happy.

WHERE HAVE YOU TRAVELED?

I've been to all fifty states and met some really cool young people in all of them. I've been to England, France, Germany, Puerto Rico, Belize, Virgin Gorda, and Mexico. And probably a couple of other places I don't remember right now.

WHAT LANGUAGES DO YOU SPEAK?

Mostly English but I also know Spanish and a good bit of American Sign Language. If I am desperate, I can find a bathroom in French and German.

WHAT ARE SOME OF THE OTHER LANGUAGES YOUR BOOKS ARE PUBLISHED IN?

Italian, Dutch, Tagalog, French, Spanish, German, Japanese, Mandarin, Turkish, and a few others I don't remember right now.

IS WRITING HARD?

Yes. Anything you do that you want to do well can be difficult at times. Revising is hard. Thinking of new things to write about is hard. And the difficulty makes it that much more rewarding.

ARE ANY OF YOUR BOOKS BASED ON YOUR LIFE?

The only ones that have some autobiographical content are *Visiting Day*, *Sweet, Sweet Memory*, *Show Way*, and all the Maizon books.

DO YOU EVER GET WRITER'S BLOCK?

Nope. I don't believe there is any such thing as writer's block. I think it's just your mind telling you that the thing you're writing isn't the thing you really want to be writing. If this happens to me, I start writing something else.

DO YOU HAVE ANY KIDS?

I have a daughter named Toshi and a son named Jackson-Leroi. Toshi was named after her godmom, Toshi Reagon, who is a really cool singer.

What was your first job?

When I was a toddler, I did a series of advertisements for Alaga Syrup in *Ebony* magazine. Even though I was only two, I looked a lot older, and the ads that ran often featured me as a school-aged child thinking about Alaga Syrup. I don't remember loving it. But it was technically my first job.

What music do you listen to?

Here are some of the people on my computer: Toshi Reagon, Joni Mitchell, Kanye West, Talib Kweli, Bruce Springsteen, Black Eyed Peas, Nas, Indigo Girls, ani difranco, Eminem, and the whole *Free to Be . . . You and Me* soundtrack.

How many books do you work on at one time?

I'm usually working on two or three books at once. When I get bored with one, or get stuck, I go on to the other one.

Where do you write?

I have a writing room in my house in Brooklyn. Sometimes I go to a place called The Writers Room in Manhattan. Sometimes I sit on the stoop or write in Prospect Park. Sometimes, if an idea starts coming, I just write wherever I am and on whatever I have.

Of all the books you've written, do you have a favorite?

Nope. I like each of them for different reasons. Sometimes, long after I've finished a book, I'm still thinking about the people in them.

IF YOU COULDN'T WRITE, WHAT WOULD YOU DO?
Play for the NBA—try to make those Knicks a winning team!

DO YOU THINK YOU'LL EVER STOP WRITING?
When I stop breathing.